𝔇ark 𝔗ales
Volume XV

Edited by
Sean Jeffery

This collection first published in Great Britain in 2011 by
Dark Tales, 7 Offley Street, Worcester WR3 8BH
www.darktales.co.uk

The rights of the authors and contributors have been asserted in accordance with sections 77 and 78 of the Copyright, Designs and Patents Act 1988.

ISBN 978-0-9555104-6-5

Printed in Great Britain by the MPG Books Group, Bodmin and King's Lynn

WELCOME TO DARK TALES

"You said he was obsessed with death, Frau Kueper. But you speak of clockwork things. Machines. They do not live or die."
"Do they not?" she asked, and it was couched as an earnest question. "Then, doctor, I am surely damned."

CONTENTS

DIE KÜCHE BENJAMIN MITCHELL

The kitchen appeared through darkness beyond the door, which stood guard. The intruder's finger ignited the switch.

There was a drip.

Enter into the grey light stricken room as the fluorescent glow refuses to exert itself at full force, allowing only a quarter of the capacity it had in younger, newer, brighter days.

The neat, square, once shiny sink lays complete with faucet bleeding.

Drip by drip.

The room's clinical-ness is betrayed by the grey paint, which pulls itself from the wall as suffocated air sleeps still in the room. Time ages the room whilst the Formica table stands in the middle mockingly.

Imagine the rust riding the first flow of water which journeys with a jolt from the water's outlet.

All that exists now is this room. Outside it, is nowhere, the unknown, unknowable and incomplete.

The room never moves, it sits pathetically still to watch events unfold within, never knowing the whole story, only its own separate but continual happenings; it reacts with its visitors but remains motionless.

The frosted windows tell untruths of another place, an outside, an "out there", though it's nothing but hope or a dream.

A visitor enters. The room acts only as it can, awaiting intervention.

Its wooden floors enjoy the impact of the visitor's feet, arching, bowing, creaking as they vocalise the forgotten act. Dust from the floor realises its chance to migrate, attaching itself to the moist feet that trample it. The faucet takes the opportunity to drip once again only to remind itself that it's still there. Crumbs surround the obvious places, around the stove, between the sink and bench, and in front of the refrigerator, where a broom sits innocently beside.

The kitchen knows "the user" for he treats it well.

Humans know the user as Arnold. The kitchen knows Arnold as the user.

The user is he who brings them to life, makes them valid, and gives them meaning and purpose.

To the user, the kitchen is eternally the same, innate and unanimated. He doesn't appreciate it or recognise their entire function. He forgets it stores his food, protects it, and cooks it. In a way it is responsible for his nourishment. It is a symbiosis.

The kitchen has its secrets, the dripping fridge, the spider in the corner and the rotting olive under the stove. These are the rumours, the gossip of the kitchen.

The Formica table is the centre of the kitchen's attention. It's he and his harem of chairs, standing there like a pimp, looking on all else.

The user hurriedly interacts and impacts with the kitchen world. Grasping the hard metal handles, pulling drawers through their casing so the tracking splinters itself as it's stretched and warmed for use. Prying open the freezer door before he disembowels it with his warm hands, excitement peaks as the appliances wait in anticipation that they may be used next. The kettle twitches, as it is filled with cool water awakening from dormancy as it starts to boil. The toaster sparks and works up its intense heat as the spongy bread is shoved inside.

Then, Quiet……..

The fact that the user has left the room makes the air tense, whispers of "will he come back?" echo through the room.

The smell of appliance-fear, toast and boiled water all converse in the air.

"Creak, boom, boom, boom." The floorboards talk of the user returning, its moans are heard down into the kitchen, though he is still out there, outside in the unknown.

The trampled dust is smudged into the cracks as the user makes his way back in. Smoke and steam now fill the room, the heat brings the atmosphere further along, closer to life, further along the evolutionary projection of the border between inanimate and animate. A chorus of clicks, pops and beeps were sung as their purpose of existence arrived.

The air shifts as further creaks are heard from afar. Another user?

The streams of air are moving for the entrance of a new being. This user brings a louder deeper tone with him. The floors stressed at a greater degree as he vaulted himself toward the fridge. Noise emanated from the beings. They took it in turn to vocalise; actions made towards the sink where the faucet had been left on, letting water escape at an alarming rate. The verboseness of the users caused a shattering tension within the room. Glasses reverberated and cutlery jingled, shell-shocked, as the users took out their rage on the benches and walls. Grappling one another, eventually ensured involvement of the table, chairs and the floor.

The kitchen remained nonetheless indifferent.

The drawer was once again opened, with tremendous force and haste as a knife was torn from the cheap plastic dividers that separated the cutlery. A knife was grasped firmly around the handle as the cold blade was forced to break skin and became at once warm and moist.

The knife was forced and twisted and slopped between organs and arteries, as one user stirred it into the other. At once it was thrust back into the air for breath before being once again forced in for another taste of red iron liquid. The knife repeatedly travelled, back and forth in a most intensive and elaborate fashion. The rest of the kitchen waited still as it was sprayed with the warm, red liquid.

The fridge's compressor screamed.

A new silence overcame the room.

The slipping sound of a body to the ground.

A thump on the floor, which shook the inhabitants of the room.

A bloodied hand grasped the cold tap and twisted until the water became silent.

Steam and smoke settled.

The door is closed.
Another secret.

# A LOVING SON									IAIN GRANT

Maximillian, the kitchen boy, cupped his hand around the flickering flame of the lit candle as he led his master towards the parlour.

"I hope you are not angry, sir," he said, his voice breaking mid-sentence. "I was frightened and she was so insistent."

"Frightened?" said Dr Ehrlichmann. "Of what?"

"She startled me, sir. Dressed as she was. And the wind."

He pushed open the parlour door and ushered the doctor inside.

Dr Ehrlichmann looked at the woman huddled in the chair by the unlit fire, the damp blanket that she still clutched about her shoulders and body, her shaking bare feet that barely touched the floor.

Maximillian swallowed his fear noisily.

"I saw her and I thought..."

"Of course, Max," said the doctor kindly. "But I know this woman. Fetch some kindling and a pot of piping hot coffee. Wake Ada if you must."

"But sir. Her feet..."

"Yes, yes, I see. All the more reason to be quick about it."

As the boy hastened from the room, Dr Ehrlichmann crossed over to the fireplace.

"Good evening, Frau Kueper." He glanced at the clock above the mantelpiece. "Or perhaps I should say good morning."

Frau Kueper looked up at him, her blue eyes ringed by wet, pale folds of sagging skin, but said nothing.

"You have not walked all the way from Wittenburg tonight, have you?" asked the doctor. "It must be five miles or more and it is bitterly cold out."

By way of reply, the woman pulled the blanket more tightly about herself.

"The boy will return soon with drink and a fresh blanket," Dr Ehrlichmann continued. "We don't want you catching your death of cold."

"I was not sure you would recognise me, sir," said the woman at last. "It has been a year or more since we last saw you."

Dr Ehrlichmann smiled warmly. He tapped the face of the clock with the knuckle of his forefinger. Its firm and precise tick echoed heavily around the parlour.

A LOVING SON   IAIN GRANT

"Your husband's workmanship is evident throughout my home. Nor do I forget hospitable friends."

"You are too kind, sir."

"Not at all," he insisted. "But what brings you here on such a night?"

Frau Kueper stared at the floor for a long time and then said, "It is my son, Jonas."

"Your son. Is he unwell?"

She flinched and twisted her head to indicate a distasteful uncertainty.

"He is a good boy and a loving son," she said fixedly, almost accusingly.

"I am sure he is," replied the doctor.

"But he has become a morbid creature this past year. Obsessed with death."

"He is a young man and developing an understanding of his place in God's creation. This is not abnormal. And I seem to recall that his aunts earn some living by attending to the dead. Laying them out and such."

And such, thought Dr Ehrlichmann disagreeably. He did not approve of Frau Kueper's spinster sisters, peddling their superstitious practices in an age of supposed enlightenment. The covering of all mirrors and clocks in the deceased's home. The plate of salt placed upon the corpse's chest. The ribbon tying the big toes together. The killing of any cats or dogs that might enter the room where the corpse lay. The two day vigil over the body and the procession of locals in which all must touch the body, in case any of them turned out to have played a part in the death and which would be revealed through fresh, spontaneous bleeding. All nonsense, which Dr Ehrlichmann reviled utterly.

"Your son cannot help but be influenced a little by them. He has kept vigil with them on occasion perhaps?"

"Never," said Frau Kueper. "Niklas would not allow it. He had Jonas put to work in his workshop from an early age."

"Well, yes. It is good that a lad learn his father's trade."

"Perhaps," said the woman doubtfully. "He does have a talent for clockwork. My mother did say he had a greater affinity for springs, cogs, gears and chains than for other people."

"Again, this is not unusual."

"You do not understand. There was this bear-"

Frau Kueper broke off as the kitchen boy entered the room, a bundle of sticks under his left arm and a laden silver tray in his right hand. He slid the tray onto the low table at Dr Ehrlichmann's side. The spout of the tall coffee pot steamed gently.

"Sir, Ada wishes to know if you will be requiring food."

Dr Ehrlichmann looked to Frau Kueper. She shook her head and he sensed that the mention of food caused her some physical discomfort.

"Some bread, Max. Cheese and sausage. And a fresh blanket for our guest. Leave the wood. I shall deal with it."

Maximillian bowed in understanding and, leaving the wood in the hearth, hurried out.

Dr Ehrlichmann poured thick black coffee into two cups.

"You said something about a bear?"

"A clockwork thing," said the woman. "A toy made for Jonas by his father. There was a key with which to wind it and the mechanical creature would perform a bobbing dance. Up, down, up, down. It became his most treasure possession."

She smiled a little at the recollection and returning the smile, Dr Ehrlichmann offered her one of the cups of coffee.

"No thank you, doctor," she said. "Jonas kept it at his bedside and would wind it up each night before settling to sleep."

The doctor sipped at his coffee and hissed as it burnt his bottom lip.

"I see," he said, wiping his mouth.

"And then one day it broke. I don't know how. Perhaps one of the girls dropped it or accidentally trod on it but it broke and would not work again. Jonas was inconsolable."

"Could not your husband have mended it?"

"He told the boy that to mend it would be to rebuild it from scratch. The boy was upset and there was a lesson to be learnt but he refused to learn it."

Dr Ehrlichmann crouched carefully before the hearth and with a methodical slowness, began to build the fire.

"Did he not attempt to mend it himself?"

"Not at first," said Frau Kueper. "That little bear. It was as I said. He had a greater fondness for things of clockwork than for things of flesh. His little dancing friend had died. He was not quick to violate its corpse with pins and pliers. But..."

The woman shifted uncomfortably in her seat, wincing at some sudden pain in her stomach.

"Frau Kueper, are you unwell?"

"Let me finish," she insisted. "That was when Jonas changed. He became withdrawn, uncommunicative. He would hide in his room, surrounding himself with every broken piece of clockwork that had come through the workshop. He hoarded all and any discarded components. We could hear him tinkering with them late into the night. His thirst for understanding was insatiable but he never touched the broken dancing bear."

"He wanted to perfect his skills before attempting to repair the bear."

"That was what we concluded, yes."

Dr Ehrlichmann had finished constructing a modest fire and reached up to the mantelpiece for the candle with which to light it.

"You said he was obsessed with death, Frau Kueper. But you speak of clockwork things. Machines. They do not live or die."

"Do they not?" she asked, and it was couched as an earnest question. "Then, doctor, I am surely damned."

Frau Kueper managed to contain the first sob but the second caught her unawares and she hid her eyes with her hand as she wept.

A LOVING SON

IAIN GRANT

"Dear woman, get a hold of yourself," said the doctor, quickly lighting the fire and setting the candle down in the hearth. "What are you crying for?"

She sniffed noisily and wiped away oily, dark tears with the back of her hand.

"I fell ill last month," she said. "A chill that went to my chest."

"And you have risked death by coming here on such a cold night?" Dr Ehrlichmann looked round. "Where is that boy? I asked him to bring a fresh blanket. I will not have you dying for want of warmth."

The wood in the grate crackled and spat as the flames took hold. The light shone in Frau Kueper's eyes.

"I was confined to my bed for a week or more. I could not move. I could barely breathe. Father Bauer even came, prepared to administer the last rites at any moment."

"And this was only last month?"

"Jonas sat with me throughout the week. Took to the little stool at my bedside. He remained silent for the most part. My little boy. When I was awake, he would be watching me. When I slept, I would hear the sound of him fiddling with the pieces of clockwork that he always carried with him."

"As you say, he is a loving son."

"I do not doubt that. But I misunderstood his attentions, doctor. I thought he was keeping me company, offering prayers perhaps. It was only as the week progressed and I slipped further into delirium that I conceived his true motive."

"What? What was he doing?"

Frau Kueper pursed her lips sadly.

"He had perfected those skills he thought necessary and he was waiting."

"Waiting? For what?"

With some small difficulty, Frau Kueper stood up, releasing her hold on the blanket that she had wrapped about her upper body. It fell to the floor with a soft, damp thud.

"Doctor, look."

Dr Ehrlichmann stared, his eyes held against his will to the horror that protruded from her bosom.

"Frau Kueper," he whispered.

"Can you see?" she said.

In the small still centre of his terrified mind, the doctor realised his earlier error. What he had taken to be the echoing tick of the clock above the fire place was nothing of the sort. Beneath the distended and gangrenous skin of Frau Kueper's breasts, fixed to bone and flesh with screws and neat wire stitching was a clockwork motor of polished brass. Lungs welded to a system of chains. Arteries joined by rubber tubing and rhythmically contracting bladders. A coiled spring where her heart should have been.

"Can you see what he has done for me?" wept Frau Kueper.

Ehrlichmann, shoving his fist in his mouth to contain the sickness that was sweeping through him, averted his eyes downwards and realised his second error. Maximillian had tried to warn him but he had misunderstood and only now, by the growing light of the fire, did he see.

Her feet. There was a piece of ribbon tied around each of the woman's big toes, frayed ends indicating the point at which they had once been joined together.

The Illustrated Dreams of the Ancestors   Georgina Bruce

Unke: welcoming

When dead people come back to this town they shuffle along the path behind the beach, and walk upstream on the shallow river, and they trudge past the sour smelling brewery to the gnarly banyan tree in the middle of town; and I know this because I follow the trail of lanterns which have been set out to light their way.

But I do not care for ghosts, and I cannot go where they go. So I veer away from the flickering lantern path and walk towards the karaoke place and the pachinko arcade and the Dolphin Bar, which occupy one neon-bright cul-de-sac of this town. It's quiet; the regulars all no doubt at home, arranging the artefacts on the household shrine, welcoming back dead parents, uncles, aunts; welcoming back generations of grandparents to crowd and huddle in the small house and sit cross-legged on the tatami, eating sweet porridge. This is what the dead eat.

In Tokyo the dead go hungry. They wander lost, surviving on the grass and paper that is given to keep them away. But here, in this slow small place, people are waiting for them. Families are waiting for their homecoming.

And in Tokyo, my family are watching television. My husband is asleep on the sofa, his head lolling back, probably snoring. If he woke up and saw me watching, he might fling out his hand to swat me away, or spit, or simply close his eyes. My children are sitting up, leaning forward, chasing the pictures across the screen. And I know this, because I watch them, my children, and this is what they do. Meanwhile, I work and hurry and bother, trying to mend the seams of their lives, trying to patch the leaks and cover the cracks, always whispering sorry, so sorry through my bruised mouth. They will notice, eventually, that I am not coming home, when the house splits open and the clothes stand up and walk away, and my absence will be like a blown fuse or a frozen pipe, bringing everything to a stop.

Maybe.

Travelling here, with my small blue suitcase, I take a hard seat at the back of the bus, crowded in by neat young people and fragile old ones. Everyone comes home for O-bon. The palm trees and brushed concrete shimmer in the heat, and the ocean flickers silver behind the hills, and slowly the bus empties itself out at stops along the way, the hissing doors releasing the passengers into warm or sly embraces. By the time we get on the sea road to Nago-shi, I am the only one left, and in the end we stop here, near the banyan tree, and the driver cuts the engine, and there is nowhere else to go.

I get off the bus, carrying my small, too-light suitcase, and walk to a hotel on the edge of town. The owner is a small, sharp woman. She is like a little needle.

"Good afternoon, welcome," she says, but she does not smile.

A boy of five or six runs across the lobby, picks up my little suitcase and carries it away upstairs, banging it against the side of his leg.

"My grandson," says the owner.

She tells me the room number and I walk up one flight of stairs, along a carpeted hallway, and there is my room. There is no sign of any other guests, no sound or movement in the corridor. The boy has put my suitcase in the middle of the bed and he stands by the door, waiting for me. I take a 100 yen coin from my pocket and flick it through the air towards him. He catches it between his thumb and finger, grins, and makes off, leaving the door wide open behind him, and as I move forward to push it closed, a small black cat slips into the room. It sits at the foot of the bed, and starts washing its face with a paw. It is a dainty kind of a wash. I notice its face is sore and lumpy, and even though I don't much like cats, I decide to let this one stay. I am tired of being alone and even a cat is better than nobody at all.

My room doesn't even have a television, or a mini bar. From the window there is a view of the mountain and of the forest on the mountain, and the hundreds of steps carved into its side, and the grey road that winds around it. When the dusk falls, a thousand lights bloom on the mountain path, the ghostly navigation system at work. Even ghosts can find their way home, I think, and I suddenly feel very far away, and that is when the cat speaks to me, and says in a voice as clear as a bell, *What are you doing here Izumi?*

I react with instinctive violence, terrified, hopping back on one foot and kicking the cat hard with the other. I kick it so hard that it flies across the room and hits the wall with a wet smash, sliding lifelessly to the carpet. Adrenalin stings me all over and I stand for a moment, shaking I think, but then I walk over and nudge the cat with my toe. I'm half expecting it to leap up and scratch out my eyes, but it is a bag of broken bones.

My heart is punching against my ribcage. I have never killed before, but there is something horribly familiar about the act. I feel the cat's pain and shock in my own body, like it belongs to me.

It looks awful, the dead black cat on the pale cream carpet.

So I open my empty blue suitcase, and use it to scoop the cat up, pushing it against the wall and flipping it inside. It slides around on the shiny beige fabric in the bottom of the case. I lock the suitcase, and put it under the bed, pushing it back with my foot. Then I put on my jacket and follow the lights into the town, and that is how I end up in the Dolphin Bar.

There is no one here. At one end of the bar, the bartender sits reading a book. A Nina Simone record is playing, her melancholy voice sounding thin through the tinny speakers. The bartender doesn't come to me, but waits for me to walk over to his end of the bar. I sit on a high stool and drum my fingers on the counter top. He puts his book down, splaying the pages.

"Now, what's a nice girl like you doing in a place like this?"

The bartender looks young, like a student maybe. The book is that novel by Banana Yoshimoto: Kitchen. I've read it, too, and I like that the bartender is reading it. It makes me think he must be clever. It's a clever book.

"I'm not so nice," I say. "But thanks, anyway."

"Home for O-bon?"

I shake my head. The bartender raises his eyebrows, but gives nothing of his thoughts away. I decide I like this about him. It is sometimes an act of kindness, keeping your thoughts to yourself.

"What can I get you?" he asks.

"What do you recommend?" I don't feel like deciding for myself.

"I could make you a cocktail," says the bartender. He gives me another cool, appraising look. "How about a Halloween?"

"Alright." I don't bother to ask the ingredients. As long as it contains alcohol, that's all that concerns me.

"This music okay for you?" asks the bartender, tipping ice into a silver shaker.

Nina Simone is singing *I want a little sugar in my bowl*. It makes me want to smoke, and I say so. The bartender takes a packet of Seven Stars from his shirt pocket, along with a lighter, and puts them on the bar.

"Help yourself," he says. "Unless you don't like this brand?"

"No, it's fine. Thank you."

I smoke a cigarette while the bartender mixes my drink, and I watch him. Everything about him is clever, his clever hands and his soft clever mouth. I can't help but compare him to my husband, who is older, different, further away. My husband sniffs my neck, grabs at my shoulders, says: *I know everything Izumi. Don't be stupid. You can't have secrets from me.*

"One Halloween," says the bartender, placing the drink in front of me. "All the spirits. Be careful, it's strong."

I take a tentative sip. It is sweet, which I didn't expect. I can't taste the alcohol at all.

"Very nice," I say. Then I say: "I could get drunk and sleep with you."

I don't know why I say it, it just comes out, but the bartender doesn't so much as blink. He just looks at me coolly, his head slightly tilted to one side. Nina sings put some steam in my clothes, the speakers shaking her voice.

"I'm sorry," I say. "That was unbelievably rude of me."

"Not at all," he says, taking a cigarette from the packet and lighting it. He blows out the smoke before saying, "Please don't confuse my hesitation with reluctance. Of course I want to sleep with you. It's just a little unexpected, that's all."

"No please. Sorry. I don't know why I even said it. I'm not myself at the moment."

"Oh? Then who are you?" asks the bartender. It's a reasonable question, but I cannot answer it. I shake my head, and feel the first tears spill onto my face. He puts his hand over mine, squeezes briefly.

"It'll come to you," he says.

Nakabi: feasting

After the first two hundred steps there is a dusty clearing and large stones leading up to a shrine. I do not ring the bell or make a wish. Instead I sit on the stone ledge and take a long drink of water. I'm sweating and breathless, but anyway I light a cigarette, a Seven Stars, before I carry on.

The forest sings. Crickets, frogs and snakes rustle and skitter and slide, birds chirrup and call out, tree to tree. Mice titter in the grass. The heat drags on me, pulling sweat from my scalp into my hair, down my back. After the steps there is a tarmac road, and then there is a short bridge over a deep green chasm. Far below, water runs like a silver rope through the forest. Then there is a path made of wood and bark, which meanders through the trees.

My husband would like it here. He would photograph everything, leaning over the wooden handrail, crouching in the grass. And the children would run, laughing and shouting, keeping out of his shots. Only I would be trailing behind, carrying the picnic things, the coats, the spare lens and the camera bag. Maybe there would be a small fading bruise near my eye, and the children would pretend not to notice, and my husband would warn me not to spoil their holiday.

"Your ugly little affair," he says. "Was it good, Izumi? Do you like doing it with waiters?"

And I say, "He's not a waiter. He works in a bar."

Then something breaks inside him, and I hear it snap.

But this is not what is happening. Wake up, Izumi! They are in Tokyo, in the stupid, tiny little flat, and they have not even noticed that I've gone. Maybe they think that I've been gone all this time, anyway. These few days are nothing special to them. But it's different here.

At the top of the path, finally, there is a playground, and a golf course, and a car park.

THE ILLUSTRATED DREAMS OF THE ANCESTORS   GEORGINA BRUCE

How have they done this – sawn the top off the mountain? Up here, there are families everywhere. They must have come by car, up the steep mountain road. They sit at picnic tables or on the grass, eating and drinking with their ancestors, sharing out the food between the living and the dead. And then there is me. I sit on the mossy wall of the car park and look down over the town. The distant sea is clear aquamarine, the town a web of grey cables and pylons over pale buildings.

At the first cool wisp of breeze on my skin I get up and brush grass from my skirt, and climb down past the car park onto the road. I pass a family sitting around a picnic table, and as I walk by, the little girl holds out her hands and gives me a paper plate of meat scraps and rice and grass. I try to speak to her, to say something, (*you look like my little girl*), but she turns away from me quickly. So I take the food and eat it on my way down, even the clumps of grass, which are somewhat sweet. I am hurrying to get to the bottom of the steps before the sun goes down. Big fruitbats wake up in the trees, stretching their wings, sonically testing the air, and I don't want to be out here in the darkness.

When I arrive back at the hotel, the owner is standing outside in the street. She glares at me as I approach.

"Good evening, Izumi-san," she says and bows very politely, all with the same angry scowl all over her chops. "Are you well?"

"Yes, thank you," I reply.

"I don't suppose you've seen a cat around here, have you?" asks the owner. "She usually comes for her dinner."

"Sorry," I say. "I hope you find her."

The owner glares at me again, but only briefly, before turning to scan the street once more, and whistle softly through her teeth.

In my room, I take a long shower and lie naked on the bed, in the square of pale sunlight that pours in through the window. The cat lies next to me on the pillow, blood leaking from its ear. It is growing stiff and its fur is starting to look waxy. Nonetheless, I can hear it making sweet little purring noises near my ear. Maybe some things like to be dead.

Haven't you ever heard that cats have nine lives, Izumi? We're not that easy to kill.

At once I feel embarrassed to be naked and I jump up and pull on the thin cotton yukata, tying it firmly at my waist. I don't want the cat to see my body, my scars. I feel ashamed.

Anyway, there's more than one way to be alive. And dead. Know what I mean?

The cat gets stiffly up and turns around in robotic circles, its bones making crunching, scraping noises under the fur. When it finally sits still again it is the wrong shape for a cat. It looks at me through its white eyes.

Remember what it felt like, Izumi, getting kicked that hard? Ouch.

I shake my head. I don't want to hear this.

But what are you doing here? asks the cat in its clear chiming voice. *No porridge in*

Tokyo? No feast for Izumi?

"Shut up."

I pick up my jeans from the chair and put them on, and turn my back to the cat to pull a tee-shirt over my head.

What are you doing, Izumi? We need to talk.

I put my wallet into my pocket, push my hair back into a ponytail.

Where are you going?

I slam the door behind me on the way out.

The Dolphin Bar is busier tonight. Most of the tables are full and I can't hear the music for the sound of voices. I sit at the end of the bar, smoking cigarettes, until the bartender sees me and comes over.

"You're busy tonight," I say.

He shrugs. "Sure. People come and visit their families. They spend all day with people they don't usually see for months on end. They need a drink."

I nod. "Family is a difficult thing."

The bartender only looks at me, that long look again. It's sort of embarrassing. Eventually he nods, turns around and pulls down a bottle of something from a shelf behind the bar. He puts the bottle on the counter, and next to it a large tumbler.

"Awamori," he says. "Have you ever drunk it?"

He pours some of the straw-coloured liquid into the tumbler and pushes it towards me.

"This is what the old people drink," he says. "This is the spirit of Ryukyu, these islands. You should drink this tonight."

I taste it. It's smoky, like a good whisky, but it has a sweet aftertaste. I take another sip.

"Drink," says the bartender. "I'll be back in a while."

He leaves me sitting on the high stool at the end of the bar, tumbler in my hand. I want him to come back soon. I think about what it's like to kiss him. The Awamori burns my throat, soothes my throat, burns it again. It is not long before I am in the bottle, seeing everything through a pale amber glass. When the bartender comes back, I am resting my head on the counter top, my eyes closed. He comes up behind me and lifts up my tee-shirt, putting his hands over my breasts. My body responds to his touch with a rush of warmth and desire. The bar is empty again, silent now, except for the sound of the bartender's breath on my neck, and my own breath. And then I think that he must be able to see, under my raised tee-shirt, my bare skin and the ugly white scar in the shape of a shoeprint.

"No," I say. "I'm drunk."

He stops touching me, pulls my tee-shirt back down.

"It's okay," he says. "It doesn't matter to me."

I turn to look at him, to say something, but I can't speak. I need to be sick. In the bathroom, the bartender holds back my hair while I vomit. Clumps of soil and grass come up with the Awamori, clogging sweetly in my throat. The bartender strokes my forehead and my face, gives me water to sip. After half an hour, I'm done, and I splash water onto my face and rub it dry with a towel, while the bartender cleans up around me. For a moment I feel like we are some old married couple, and I remember my husband is in Tokyo, but I'm not there anymore, and the thought of it sends the blood rushing up to the surface of my skin, like a hot flush, almost like joy.

Ukui: returning

I wake up in the hotel room, my head pounding, and the dead cat lying like a stone in the space between my neck and my shoulder. It must have slipped down off the pillow in the night. I can hardly turn my head, and I have to stand under a hot shower for several minutes until my neck finally relaxes and the headache starts to fade. I can still feel the bartender's fingers on my skin, can feel him inside me, but when I turn my attention to the feeling, it disappears. I was too drunk for sex. It didn't happen. But somehow the bartender got inside me anyway. With one of his deadly cool looks, I suppose.

Sleep well, Izumi? asks the cat. I don't like to look at it. One of its knees is bent backwards and sticks out awkwardly under its body.

I ignore the cat and finish dressing, putting my dark sunglasses on to complete the look.

I've missed breakfast, so I decide to walk into town. When I come out of the hotel, I see the owner and her grandson are on the street. The grandson sits on the kerb, playing with some small toy, while the owner paces up and down, her heels tapping on the pavement, an open tin of tuna in her hand.

"Maybe she left," I say to the owner. "Sometimes cats can be like that."

The owner grimaces and stabs a finger into the tuna. "Not this cat," she says.

"They're all the same," I tell her.

The owner shakes her head and continues pacing up and down, clicking her tongue and whistling through her teeth, and the boy lets out a high-pitched giggle. I turn to look at him and he holds up the palm of his hand, and hands something to me. It is a paper model of a bus, a long, squat bus, with windows and wheels, and even a tiny driver at the steering wheel.

"Did you make this?" I ask, but he doesn't answer.

The owner hurries over, grabs the boy by his arm and yanks him to his feet.

"Help me look for the cat," she tells the boy.

I have breakfast in a noodle shop near the banyan tree, where they serve me a perfect miso soup, but in the rice there are bits of grass and paper. I eat it, anyway, because I'm hungry, and because it doesn't taste bad to me, even though I think maybe it should. I leave coins on the counter, because they will not take the money from my hand.

The bartender is waiting for me outside the shop.

"It's my day off," he says. "I went to your hotel. I've been looking for you."

I turn my head away to hide my smile. I'm glad he is here.

There is a small museum not far from the banyan tree, and we walk there. It is free to go inside, and it is very cool in the rooms, and there is no one else there. We stand for a long while looking at photographs of men and women wading in the sea, spearing sharks at their feet in the frothing ocean. Some of the spears are in glass boxes in the middle of the room.

"Your ancestors," I say to the bartender, gesturing to the photographs, and he nods.

"My family," he says.

There is another room upstairs, and in that room there is a cabinet full of paper sculptures. There are houses, ships, cars, computers, flowers and jewellery and mobile phones, all made of paper.

I take the paper bus from my pocket and place it on top of the cabinet. The bartender picks it up again, and turns it over in his hands.

"You made this?" he asks.

I shake my head. There is a notice on the display cabinet, explaining that the sculptures were made by local schoolchildren, as examples of the traditional gifts to the dead.

"These paper models are not for burning," the bartender reads aloud to me, "but to demonstrate the living traditions of our island."

"On the mainland, they burn money," I say.

"Yes, yes, that's the Japanese way. This is the Okinawan way. It's different here. More tradition. More belief. Here we give the dead everything: cars, telephones, suitcases, houses, record players, everything they need."

I nod, and then I say, "What happens if no-one believes in you?"

The bartender takes my hand in his. "It must be very lonely," he says. He smiles. "But we're always here, dreaming of them and their world, and they're probably wherever they are, dreaming about us."

"The dreams of the ancestors," I say.

"Maybe that's all we are," says the bartender, giving me another of his deadly looks, and squeezing my hand.

"I have a husband," I tell him. "There are some problems. I want to be honest with

THE ILLUSTRATED DREAMS OF THE ANCESTORS   GEORGINA BRUCE

you."

He shakes his head and says, "I understand. But it doesn't matter to me." Then he smiles again and says, "I never forgot about you, Izumi. You see that now, don't you?"

I cannot answer. There are words in my fingers, touching his, and I hope he can hear them.

We part underneath the banyan tree, saying nothing much to one another. I stare at his face, trying to memorise that look of his, but it's impossible, and in the end I stand on tiptoes to kiss his cheek, and turn away before he can say anything.

In my hotel room, I sit by the window and the cat drags its lumpy body over to me and attempts to climb into my lap, until I finally take pity on it and pick it up. It settles on my knees, cracking its neck to look up at me.

"Everyone's looking for you," I say.

I expect they'll find me somehow, says the cat. *But what about you?*

"It doesn't matter," I say. "I might just stay here."

You can't stay here, Izumi. It doesn't work like that. There isn't anything here.

"You're here. I'm here."

Me? A dead cat that talks. Yeah, right, Izumi. Sure. And you. What are you, now?

"I don't have to answer that," I say.

I'm sorry about it, says the cat, *but no one recovers from a kick like that. You can see for yourself.*

The black cat rolls on its side in my lap, and I see the misshapen bones shift under its skin.

Are you dreaming or being dreamed? How did you get to be so lost, Izumi?

And I realise that I do not know. Maybe because there was no one to call me home or light my way. Maybe because my husband does not want to be haunted by me, because he cannot stand it, and my children are too young, they can't remember my face, and there is no one with a lantern at twilight to lead me into a house and feed me sweet porridge.

"Maybe I'm not lost," I tell the cat. "Maybe I've been found."

In the drawer of the dresser there is paper, thin grey paper. I take a sheet and start to fold it and twist it into the shape of a banyan tree. I get scissors and Sellotape, too, and start to make other things. A mountain with a flat top, a small hotel, a bar, carefully cutting the shapes and sticking them together, but anyway ending up with small torn things. I set them all out on the dresser, trying to make the shape of the town. All the while, the cat watches me and clear fluid drips from its mouth onto my jeans, but I do not mind.

I make a man, a kind young man, and I try to draw his face, with its odd disarming gaze, but I am clumsy at drawing and I cannot get it right. I make other people too, and bats, and a cat, and a forest. I can't stop. I draw windows on the houses, neon lights on the pachinko arcade. Finally, when it is already getting dark outside, and the paper is all used up, I think it will do. I think I have enough.

One by one, I put the paper things into my small suitcase. When I walk down to the street, the boy is out there already, with matches in his hands. He takes my suitcase and puts it in the middle of the road, on the shallow bump in the tarmac, and puts the box of matches on top. I flick a coin over to him, which he catches in his thumb and forefinger, then, kneeling, I open the case.

The small black cat springs out and leaps past me in a rush of fur and claws. Alive, again, running home to the music of its hunger. The boy sees it, turns and runs after it into the hotel, calling his grandmother to come.

Further down the street, small fires are already burning. A scrap of paper money floats past my ear.

I wonder if I should have said goodbye properly to the bartender, but then I think maybe this is the right way, after all. Maybe he is burning paper bottles outside the Dolphin Bar.

The paper catches as soon as I put the match to it. Smoke fills my nostrils. The paper bus is burning, and I feel its wheels turning under me, carrying me away. It will carry me back to Tokyo, some kind of Tokyo anyway. It is good to go back, because I must. I have to dream these things for my children, keep dreaming them a world they can live in, keep believing in their world even though it no longer believes in me. They are my children, after all, and I must do what I can for them. I'll be their ghost.

But I won't go back empty as I came. The paper town is burning, the banyan tree and the Dolphin Bar. Next year, I call out as I leave, hoping he will hear me: next year, I'll dream you again.

Copyright © Georgina Bruce 2011

BE SEEING YOU   KEITH MELTON

She had been dead for two hours when she smiled at me. No pleasure in the smile—something almost predatory lingered in the curve of teeth, yellow now in the arc sodium light streaming through the windshield, and I had to look away.

My driver-side window was part-way down, and I could smell wet asphalt and blood. Insects tap-tap-tapped against the grimy, warped plastic that enclosed the light on the motel wall. Tap. Tap. Tap-tap. Relentless. Driven. Mindless.

The dead woman grabbed the handle on the armrest and pulled herself out of her slouch. The rope-thin muscle in her bicep hardened beneath her skin, making me think of worms tunnelling in loose soil. I licked my teeth with my tongue. They felt dirty, scummy. I hadn't brushed them in a while and they made me uncomfortable, but I tried not to think about it too much.

"You're still here," the dead woman said. Her voice buzzed like a cracked clarinet reed. Her smile had vanished. Black, dilated pupils, now frozen in place. Her lips already blued, nightshade lipstick that made her skin even more jaundiced in the yellow light.

"I can't leave yet," I said, very softly. But her dark eyes remained fixed on me, staring unblinking with the flat gaze of a snake. Her young face held no expression, appearing as it had in the hours before her smile, when she was silent, and I was thinking.

"What do you want?" she asked.

"Is there still pain?" Anything to change the subject. I even missed the smile, as disconcerting as it had been.

"No." Blood had soaked her blouse, leaving only her white sleeves unstained. The blood was black and thick from her throat to her jeans. It made me think of chocolate covered cherries. Chewed up chocolate covered cherries that someone had spit back out. I looked away again, back toward the moths.

I couldn't do this anymore.

Still, I took out the narrow pen case and set it on my knee. My leather journal came next, and I opened it and set it on my lap. The pages were yellowed, ancient parchment in the light from the motel. I took the gold pen out of the case. It always felt surprisingly heavy in my fingers. Incongruous. Like a dead woman's smile.

Only one other car sat in the back of the motel lot with us. It was a chain motel with beige stucco walls and rows of red doors stretching away from me like an artist's exercise in perspective. I took a deep breath, smelling the blood, smelling my sweat. It had rained an hour ago, but now the rain had stopped. The constant hiss-rumble of freeway traffic drifted from the overpass.

"I have a few questions," I finally said. I twisted the gold pen, watching the spike tip peek its head out. A fang filled with ink instead of venom.

"Why?" she asked.

I didn't answer. Gently, I paged past the other entries where my handwriting scrolled in line after line of neat capital letters. No dates, too dangerous, but line after line of the purest things, the ideas crystalline, an intimacy so profoundly beyond the physical that my hands trembled. No time now to read them again and savour them. I turned to an empty page in the notebook and smoothed it flat. My skin rasped against the paper and left a smear of red across the surface.

"What's your name?" I said.

I waited a long moment, looking at the blank notebook page, feeling her stare prickle across my skin like centipede feet. She wasn't going to answer. I wrote down the name Chloe, because there was something about the way the name looked on paper that I'd always liked.

"Why?" she asked again, and I looked up from the notebook, looked at her perfect cupid-bow lips. Watched for the smile that didn't come.

"What are you happy to escape?" I said, pressing on as if she hadn't spoken. But she still didn't answer. "What did you hate the most?" Hoping a reword would spur something.

Another long silence. I waited her out.

"Driving..." she said. I wrote down the word, waiting for more. "Driving behind... driving behind someone slow..." Her mouth moved silently for a second, as if her words were sub-audible. "Someone slow who suddenly speeds up to run a yellow light. Leaving me at the red. That."

I wrote it all down, my gold pen skating across the paper arranging neat lines of perfectly slanted capital letters. Strange, the things people said when I asked that question. In a world of Hitlers, Enrons and Darfur, they always gave me a personal hate. Spitting it up like bile. And it was always some little thing. Some stupid little thing.

I swallowed and my throat made a little click. My mouth was dry as I prepared myself for the next question, holding my pen ready in my hand. Not holding too hard. Too hard and I'd dent impressions from the pen into my fingers, and my hand already ached from when the handle of the knife had bitten into my fingers.

"What will you miss the most?" I asked.

Her gaze wandered over to the moths for a moment, then slid back to me, seemed to linger somewhere around my throat, considering.

"Snow," she said. Her words were soft, almost a sigh. "Snow on cold Sunday mornings. Me in bed, wrapped in a million blankets. Warm. The scrape of snowploughs on the streets. A white sheet of snowfall drifting down. And me, warm. Warm in my bed."

I wrote it all down. Every word. And when silence replaced the scritch of my pen tip across the paper, I carefully put the pen back into its case and slowly closed the lid. I shut the notebook and turned to look at her. "Anything else?" I asked, already knowing the answer.

She gave a slight shake of her head.

"Then it's time," I said.

Her thin fingers popped open the door and she climbed out of the car. She shut the door behind her, and for a moment I sat alone. Gently, I ran my hand over the tattered steering wheel, feeling the rough texture, thinking about her answers. The goddamn warm blankets. I'd wanted that one.

I stepped out of the car, and the door *skreeked* when I swung it shut. The sound of rushing water was much louder out here, and I looked to my right, into the darkness beyond the reach of the yellow motel lights. The stream ran wide and swift, flowing

beneath the overpass where the blackberries had grown unchecked. Traffic whooshed and roared above me on the overpass. The occasional Morse-code stutter of lights blinked above the railing as a semi rushed past.

The dead woman walked away from the car, not waiting for me, heading across the parking lot toward the stream and the overpass. Her feet were small. The heels of her canvas shoes were white, very white. They made me think of snow.

I followed her, over the curb at the edge of the lot, the cement barrier marking the end of white-lined symmetry and the beginning of the riot and tangle of weeds, ivy, blackberry bushes, reeds and trees. The massive concrete pillars holding up the overpass thrust down into the greenery, pinning down the chaos. I peered into the shadowed beams forty feet overhead. When I placed my hand on a pillar I could feel the vibration as traffic rushed by. A hypnotic tremor.

An overgrown path led down from the parking lot to the rocks at the edge of the stream. She climbed down the path, only a little way ahead of me. I wanted to touch her hair, but I didn't. The time for that was gone.

She lay down in the water. The stream wasn't deep, a foot or so high at most, running swiftly past the reeds and the thorn whips of the blackberry bushes. Lights from the streetlamps and the buildings reflected downstream on its onyx surface, wavering in the ripples.

Her hair spread out around her like a halo in the water. She floated there, staring up at me with her dark eyes. So horribly wounded. I could barely bring myself to look at her, she was so beautiful.

The icy cold water soaked everything from my shins down, making me grit my teeth. I bent down and gave her two coins. Two of those gold dollar coins with the woman and child on them, pressing them into her hand. Closing her fingers around them. Laying her hand on her chest, the cold water biting at my skin. I couldn't bring myself to put the coins on her eyes. The thought of touching those staring eyes made my stomach clench, my chest feel full of freezing water.

"I'll be seeing you," she whispered, and sudden malice frosted her smile like a sickle blade. The current caught her, pulling her gently downstream. Her eyes still held that same patient, calculating predator stare, but it was too late to cover them with the coins. My mistake. A stupid weakness, and now, perhaps, she would be watching for me.

She drifted away, her face free of the dark water. One hand closed around the coins. One hand open and floating.

I could still feel her uncovered eyes staring at me.

She drifted down into the darkness beyond the reeds. My heart beat hard against my ribcage, and my stomach felt full of churning acid. *I'll be seeing you*. A promise.

A frog croaked in belligerent competition with crickets. I bent down again, the muscles in my thighs aching as if I'd bruised them. Slowly, carefully, I washed my hands in the icy water. Snow run-off. At first it hurt, but I kept my hands beneath the water until they numbed and the new pain was indistinguishable from the old.

My boots whispered against the weeds and the tangled, wet ivy as I climbed the embankment. The whisper returned to flat, echoing footsteps when I stepped back onto the asphalt. I walked to the car, remembering her words, all of them, not just those last.

One day, maybe soon, I'd ask the questions of myself... or someone, maybe the dead woman, would ask them of me. And would I float so serenely then? And what would my own answers be?

I sat in the car, the window still cracked, and listened to the moths. Tap. Tap. Tap-tap.

Kate Measom   The Wolf Runs in the Barley

"The wolf runs in the barley," Nana Hilda used to say.

Those long hazy summers of my youth were the kind of cotton wool memories I should have been able to look back on with fondness. Nana Hilda standing at the bottom of our garden, leaning on the fence and puffing on those slim brown cigarettes that were never far from her lips, her salt and pepper old-lady perm and that suggestion of a moustache balancing on her top lip which I could never quite take my eyes off.

She was an odd shape, Nana Hilda, like the tiers of a wedding cake collapsed on top of one another. I remember she always wore an apron about her waist, even in the evening when the cooking and cleaning were over for the day. She was the kind of Nana that made me the envy of my friends, and on those balmy July evenings I'd join her by the fence, looking out across the barley fields.

"The wolf runs in the barley," she'd tell me with an absent flick of her cigarette. "Don't you be playing in that field now missy, or 'e'll get you 'e will," she'd nod.

I used to laugh and think no more of it; that it was just one of those strange things grandparents said, like carrots making you see in the dark. Even at the tender age of six I knew there were no wolves in Charnwood Forest.

Summers were long when I was a child, stretching from early May to late September, and my fair freckled skin was forever blushed red from those ice cream days of innocent play. I was so many people back then – the cowboy, the nurse, the one who was 'it' in hide-and-go-seek. Now I was nobody. Gone. Forgotten. The wolf runs in the barley, Nana Hilda used to say.

I remember that first day when the proverbial penny dropped. I was kneeling on my bed and gazing out the window at a beautiful sunset that bathed the sky in a crimson flush, criss-crossed here and there with jet plume feathers. Nana Hilda was in the familiar spot by the fence, chain-smoking in a haze of blue. And then I saw it.

It was a marvel that I hadn't noticed before. A wave rippled through the sandy stalks like a winding road to nowhere. I pressed my finger against the windowpane and followed that wave, tracing a greasy pattern on the glass. Nana Hilda saw it too. She watched as it weaved its way through the field in a giddy dance, and I knew then that it was just the wind.

I was always somehow disappointed when the farmer took my barley away and replaced that yellowy swathe with ugly rows of turnips. Those hideous, hobgoblin roots acted as a marker in my life, a turning of the season in my childhood, and when finally the barley returned I was older, less mesmerised from afar by its beauty and more inquisitive to roam amidst the golden stalks in search of the secrets they held.

I remember that first terrible thrill of excitement as I clambered over the fence, faltering only momentarily before the addictive drive of adventure took over, and I plunged into the swaying forest, laughing with delight as I all but disappeared amongst the towering cereal army. The interchanging sensations of scratch and tickle rippled over my bare legs as I ran, the tightly packed stalks protesting at my invasion as I punched my way across the field. When exhaustion took hold and the mid-summer's heat sapped the fire from my muscles, I collapsed on a bed of barley and lay gasping like a fish out of water, until the first dozy tendrils of sleep came in an ectoplasmic possession. Through half drawn eyelids I watched the cirrocumulus drift across the cornflower sky, picture framed in whispering gold. The world seemed so at peace and I rested in the luxury of a listless slumber, sung to sleep by a lullaby created of breeze through crop.

It was dusk when I awoke, cold and uncomfortable. A familiar voice was calling to me through the pea soup of sleep. Using her voice as a guiding beacon in the dark, I eventually emerged by the garden fence beneath Nana Hilda's furious glare.

"What did I tell you, you stupid girl?" she fumed, almost dragging me over the fence by the sleeve of my tee-shirt. "I told you about 'im, about the wolf. Now 'e's seen you. 'E's got your scent and 'e won't rest until 'e entices you back into that there field!"

"But Nana," I protested, stumbling up the garden path as she prodded me along with a gnarled arthritic finger. "There are no wolves, not really."

"The wolf runs in the barley," she said emphatically. "Now get up those stairs and don't let me catch you in that field again."

Blushed scarlet with shame, I rubbed at my tear-stained cheeks and embarked on an early bed time. I didn't sleep easily that night. My afternoon nap and Nana Hilda's scolding combined to leave me wide awake, and I sat by the window for much of the night, watching the current of the night breeze trace conduits and alleyways through the barley, weaving, winding, twisting and turning until I was half hypnotised by the myriad patterns.

It was a good while before I got into that field again. A dutiful sentry, Nana Hilda guarded the fence like a rabid pit-bull, just falling short of snarling at me when my gaze wandered westward to the swaying golden ocean. Indeed, she succeeded in spoiling my entire summer, for before I had the chance to step foot amongst the barley ears, autumn was upon us and the farmer rotated his crops once more. And so I waited, biding my time in the hope that a future summer would bring with it the opportunity for me to run with abandonment through the field of gold.

It was with some surprise that Nana's wolf became the subject of conversation whilst my mother was carving the Christmas turkey. I'd always known of the dreadful scar on Nana's right arm, yet the sneering red grimace was merely a familiar part of her, like the evermore visible moustache on her lip or the vivid blue curlers she wore beneath the old paisley headscarf when she went to bed. Our household was inevitably plunged into chaos during the festive period and this year was no exception. There was such a clutter of aunts, uncles, cousins and friends that nobody seemed to notice me when I entered the steam-filled kitchen.

"Why doesn't she have it removed?" cousin Shelley asked my mother, spooning steaming sprouts into a colander and wobbling ever so slightly from the effects of a mid-morning tipple.

"Oh, she says she's too old for such vanity," Mum replied, loading plate after plate

THE WOLF RUNS IN THE BARLEY   KATE MEASOM

with succulent slices of turkey breast.

"Oh nonsense," Shelley scoffed. "The old bird's loaded. After all, she can't take it with her."

I hadn't known what she'd meant by that at the time. Now I knew all too well.

"I've told her much the same," Mum replied. "But she won't have it. She says it's a reminder."

"Of what?"

"Oh you know – that silly warning she gives to the kids, about the wolf in the back field?"

"Does she still go on about that?"

Mum rolled her eyes. "Incessantly."

"She'd do better to tell them the truth, that it was an accident."

"Oh, I know but you know old people – stuck in their ways and all. She means well, I suppose."

Cousin Shelley nodded absently and the conversation came to a close, yet my curiosity continued to simmer and when the opportunity presented itself, I didn't waste time in taking it.

Nana Hilda was standing on the back porch, shivering against the biting winter air, yet forcing her quivering hands to lift the cigarette to her lips regardless. The rest of the house was silent, littered with snoozing bodies, some inebriated, others suffering the effects of overeating. My father would call them 'podged'. Uncle Bob appeared to be a combination of the two and I'd sought the solace of the kitchen to escape some of his rather unpleasant bodily functions.

"Now what you doing in 'ere, missy?" Nana Hilda smiled, taking one last puff before stubbing her cigarette out on the doorframe and flicking it into the blackness of the night. "You'll catch your death in 'ere. Go and get in front of that fire, silly girl."

Ignoring her concerns in my quest for information, I remained in my seat at the kitchen table and asked the burning question. "Nana Hilda, how did you get that scar on your arm?"

She faltered on her path towards the living room and frowned at me, confused at my abstract question. "Now why would you want to know that?" she asked.

"I just wondered, that's all. Mum said it was an accident."

"It was no such thing!" she snapped indignantly. "It were the wolf what done it. I told 'er same as I tells you all and yet you never believe me. That damned wolf."

"But Nana, there is no wolf. It's just a story you tell to keep us from the field."

"Ay, and little good it did you last summer," she chastised. "I was once like you, you know? A little girl, all innocence and freckles and pigtails. And that field called to me, it did. Called to me with its secrets and intrigued me with those same patterns I see's you watching from up there in your room. And one day I went into that field and I ran through the barley like the devil himself was on my heels. And then I met 'im. The wolf.

And this is what 'e did to me. Left 'is mark, 'e did. I was lucky to get out of there alive. So let this be a warning and we'll say no more on the matter, my girl."

Flashing me a look that signalled an unambiguous conclusion to the conversation, she shuffled off in search of the warmth and comfort of the living room and I made my way to bed.

A strange occurrence of events happened that spring. I got my first period and my entire life seemed upended in a tornado of embarrassment and confusion. My body began to change, and with it the childhood innocence that fuelled my captivation of the barley field began to diminish. I knew that time was short, that such candid trivialities would soon be the stuff of memory. And then Nana Hilda got sick.

My parents said she'd gone to a 'home'. I didn't really understand what they meant. I didn't see what was wrong with our home but it meant that we had to move, and by late June the 'for sale' sign was being hammered into the front lawn.

Of course I had to do it. This was my last chance, my one opportunity to visit that peaceful playground and scamper uninhibited through the barley, intoxicated with the exhilaration of utter freedom.

No longer barred by the watchful eye of Nana Hilda, I bounded over the fence and ploughed into the crop, a human scythe cutting random patterns like the wind devils of my memories. I laughed out loud and danced beneath the crystal skies, my senses soaking in every minor detail to store as nostalgia that would last me a lifetime.

And then I met him.

Lounging amongst the crops and lost in the muddled thoughts of an eleven year old girl, the rhythmic tramp of footfalls on straw carried to me too late and suddenly he was there above me, all snarls and slaver, wild eyed with cruel intent.

"Hello," he said. "I knew you'd come."

Paralysed with fear, I could do no more than stare back at him, desperately forcing a scream that wouldn't come. He was taller than me, so much taller, and as sturdily built as my father. His blue plaid shirt was torn in places, stuck here and there with tufts of barley. Rust-stained jeans hung loose on his hips, held only by a length of rope that served as a crude belt.

"My name is Wolf," he said, bearing down upon me as I whimpered in dreadful resignation.

For though his basic shape was familiar, I knew this was no human. From where his fingernails should have been curved great, yellowed claws. The lower part of his face was greatly protruded into a snout-like mound, where pincer-like jaws and razor teeth were hungering to tear flesh from bone.

The house stood empty for years afterwards. I was filled with melancholy to look upon it, sad and derelict for so long, the laughter of childhood play a mere ghostly echo of times gone by. Yet time moved on, and with it came a new family, a couple and their three young children. A pretty little thing with flaxen locks and the deepest pools of blue for eyes sits in that very same spot and gazes out of the window at the barley field. I

THE WOLF RUNS IN THE BARLEY   KATE MEASOM

know what she's thinking and what she plans to do when nobody is around to see. I know that she's spellbound by the many weaving patterns in the sighing field of gold. But she doesn't see what I saw so long ago. Now there are two invisible forces painting random paths, duelling with each other and vying for that little girl's attentions.

The wolf runs in the barley.

And now, so do I.

BLACKOUT   PAUL JOHNSON-JOVANOVIC

David opened his eyes and gasped. Blackness surrounded him. Enveloping him like an invisible coffin. Afternoon light should have been spilling through the curtains to his right, through the narrow gap under the doorway to his left. But it wasn't. There was … nothing.

Darkness complete.

Blackout.

Lying in bed, his naked body flushed hot with panic, his skin prickled with gooseflesh. With his right hand resting on his chest, he could feel the panicked rise and fall of his breathing.

All he could think was, *What the fuck is going on?*

Quite often he would take an afternoon nap, a few hours siesta. Upon waking, he would always hear the same things: the beautiful sounds of birds singing their harmonious chorus; the faint, distant drone of traffic; next door's dog barking. Now, however, he could hear nothing. Not a thing.

Propping himself up on his elbows, he closed his eyes … opened them … closed them … opened them …

Reaching out, he felt around for his mobile phone, which he knew he'd left on the bedside table. His fingertips glided across the polished surface until he located it. Then he picked it up and flipped it open. It bleeped. The display should have lit up a vibrant blue, but it didn't.

Once again he thought, *What the fuck is going on? Am I blind? Surely I can't have lost my sight.* Please *God don't let me be blind. There has to be some logical explanation for this; I can't have just lost my sight, not without any warning signs. My vision was perfect before this, damn it! Why is this happening to me?*

The light switch! He had to locate the light switch. Pushing the duvet back, he pulled himself up and sat on the edge of the bed. He got to his feet, the plush carpet tickling his toes. Using the bed to guide him, he made his way across the room. Feeling along the wall, he soon found the circular dial of the dimmer. It made a dull snapping sound as he pressed it.

The room remained dark.

Pitch black.

He turned it from side to side, pressed it again. Nothing.

Balling his hands into fists, he rubbed his eyes frantically with his knuckles. He whimpered.

"I'm blind,' he said blankly. "I'm … *blind!*"

Trying hard to compose himself, he took a deep breath and moved back towards the bed. With one hand on the wooden frame, he made his way towards the window. The curtains felt silky smooth to touch. One in each hand, he steeled himself for the inevitable. They made a *swishing* sound as he flung them open. And saw nothing.

That was when his mobile rang. Making his way back to the bedside table, he felt around for the phone, quickly locating it and picking it up. Flipping it open and running his index finger across the keypad, he found the accept button, pressed it, and cupped the phone to his ear.

"David? Is that you?"

It was his girlfriend, Sandra. Never had he been so relieved to hear her voice. He sat down on the bed and, with his free hand, pulled the duvet round his shoulders to keep himself warm.

"Yeah, it's me, honey," he replied, his voice quivering. "Where are you? You've got to come home now. I can't see a thing. I think I've gone ... I think I've gone bli –"

From the other end of the phone, David thought he could hear someone scream. Faint, distant, but definitely a scream. He shuddered.

"Honey, are you still there?" he asked.

A pause, then she answered, "Yes, I'm still here." She began to cry. "I'm scared ... *so* scared."

"Why? Why are you scared? And did I just hear someone scream?"

Another pause, a sniffle, and then she explained, "I was walking up Wyvern Street, on my way back to work after a late lunch, when *it* happened. One minute the sun was shining. I can remember squinting, it was so bloody bright, and then it went dark. All of a sudden, it just went dark and I couldn't see a thing ..." She trailed off, began to sob.

"It's all right, sweet heart," David said. "Don't worry, everything's going to be okay."

He had never felt so helpless before. The woman that he loved with all of his heart needed his help and there wasn't a thing he could do. And, of course, there was his family and friends. Were they in the same predicament? Were they all now fumbling around in the dark, wondering what the heck had happened?

David felt numb.

Sandra resumed. "People started screaming. I heard the screech of brakes. Cars crashing. It was chaos. In the distance, I heard a *massive* explosion. I think a plane's gone down, David. I don't know what to do. What shall I do?"

"It's important that you just stay put, all right. Just stay put and I'll come and get you ... somehow I'll come and get you."

"Staying put could be a bit of a problem, I'm afraid. Something near to me is burning. I can hear the crackle of the flames and smell the smoke. I'm safe for now, but ..."

"Listen, you need to get away from that fire now!" he said, concerned. "That could be anything burning. It could explode at any time. Move away from the warmth, *and quickly!*"

"Okay."

He could hear her heels tapping as she walked; hear her swearing as she stumbled.

"Be careful," he said.

"I'm trying."

Something occurred to him. "How have you managed to call me? If you can't see, how have you managed to use your mobile?" As soon as the words had left his lips, he realised what a silly question it was.

"Oh come on, David, you know me; I can text with my eyes shut. I know my mobile inside out. I knew your name was fifth in my phonebook, so I ..."

"Are you away from that fire?"

"Yes."

"Are you all right?"

"Yes, but I can hear someone groaning, a woman calling for help. It sounds like she's in a lot of pain. What shall I do? Shall I try and help?"

Without being able to see, David didn't know how she could help. "I think you should just stay put, wait till I get there and then we'll both try and help."

"But it could take you hours to get he –"

The line went silent.

"Sandra?"

Silence.

"Sandra, are you there? Talk to me, honey!"

"Yes, I'm here, but ..."

"What's wrong?"

"Nothing. I thought I felt something brush past me, that's all. What do you think has happened? Why is it so dark?"

"Oh God, I wouldn't even like to hazard a guess. Who knows, maybe we've all been struck blind, but I don't think so. I don't know why, but I just get the feeling that ..."

Suddenly, from the other end of the phone, David heard a blood-curdling scream.

"Sandra," he said, "who was that? What's happening?"

"I ... I think it was the woman who was groaning, calling for help. I think someone's attacking her. Oh David, I don't know what to do. I don't know what to ..."

"Move away! Get away from there! *QUICK!*"

He heard Sandra gasp in terror. Then scream.

"What's wrong? What's going on?"

"Something j-just brushed past me."

Before David could reply, she screamed again, this time getting full soprano strength. He had to hold the phone away from his ear.

"Something just brushed against my arm." She sobbed. "Cold. It felt cold and ... *scaly!* And I can hear something, too. It sounds like ... like chattery teeth. I don't like this, David. Please come and get me. *Please* come and get me now!"

David stood up, the duvet sliding off his shoulders. "I'm going to get dressed and leave straight away, all right ..."

Another scream, then, "There's more than one of them. I think they're surrounding me ..."

The line went dead.

"*Sandra!*" David yelled. "*Sandra, talk to me! For fuck's sake, talk to me!*"

Not wanting to waste any more time, he flipped the phone shut and felt around for the clothes that he'd thrown over the end of the bed a few hours before. Just a short time before, when the world had been as it should have been, when he had fallen asleep with a smile on his face knowing that the love of his life had agreed to marry him.

To David, it felt like God had just reached out and flipped the universal light switch, finally washing his hands of humanity. Could that really be the case? he wondered. He had no time for speculation, however; he had to get moving. And fast.

Getting dressed – normally the most mundane and simple of tasks – was not proving to be easy. He had located his boxers and socks, slipping them on with no problems, but putting his jeans on was turning out to be something of a Krypton Factor challenge. First, he had put them on the wrong way round, then after realising his folly, taking them off and putting them back on again, he had caught his skin in the zip. After wrestling with it for a few seconds, he soon realised that securing his privates wasn't something he should worry about. After all, who was going to see him? He put his t-shirt and jumper on with no trouble, not caring if they were back to front.

Once again using the bed for guidance, he moved towards the bedroom door. Reaching it, he felt around for the handle. The door creaked as he pulled it open. He stepped out onto the landing.

As he got ready to tackle the stairs, his thoughts were of Sandra. She had told him that something with scaly, cold skin had touched her. She had told him that 'they' were surrounding her – things with chattery teeth. He tried to think of a logical explanation for what she'd said, for the way she had panicked. He tried to convince himself that somehow she had got it wrong, that the trauma of being suddenly plunged into a world of darkness had made her paranoid, maybe even delusional.

But if that was the case, then why hadn't she rung back?

And, of course, there was the blood-curdling scream.

Trying to call her back on his mobile wasn't an option; he knew it could take him hours to locate her number in his phonebook. Hell, writing a text when he could actually see was enough of a challenge.

He was nearly at the bottom of the stairs now, one hand on the banister, being careful but trying to move as quickly as possible. Falling and breaking a leg wasn't an option, not if he wanted to get to Sandra.

Slowly, he took the last few steps. Safely reaching the bottom, he stood there for a moment, head cocked to one side, listening. He thought he could hear something. Faint, distant, it sounded like ... chattery teeth.

"Just get a move on," he muttered to himself. "Get your arse moving!"

The porch was straight ahead. Holding his hands out in front of him, he made his way towards the front door, running one hand along the wall for guidance. Unfortunately, he had forgotten about the mirror. His hand clipped its edge and it a made a clattering sound as it slid down the wall, breaking into a thousand shards as it hit the laminate floor.

"*Shit!*"

Before he had even had a chance to try and sweep the glass aside with his foot, from outside, he could hear movement, scurrying, like the noise had attracted some unwanted attention.

"What the ...?"

Leaning forward, with one hand on the wall to steady himself, he reached out and felt around for the door handle. He opened the door. Taking a big stride, he stepped over the broken bits of mirror and entered the porch. The chattering increased to a mindbending pitch, like what was on the other side of the glass was excited by the sight of its quarry. David put his hands over his ears.

Had it not been for Sandra, he would never have contemplated going outside. But the one person who he treasured above all others was out there. And she needed his help. He had *no* choice.

The chattering subsided. As David removed his hands from his ears, he could hear another sound: like something was sucking on the glass, trying to get to him.

He bent down and felt around for his trainers. The floor was littered with footwear – mostly Sandra's – so he was lucky to find them quickly. Not bothering to mess about untying the laces, he tugged them on and went back into the house. The bits of mirror scrunched underfoot as he made his way towards the kitchen, which was to his right.

Entering the kitchen, he put one hand on the marble worktop. One, two, three steps along and then he stopped. By his reckoning, the drawer with carving knives in should have been right in front of him. It was. Opening the drawer, and being careful not to cut himself, he felt around for the biggest one he could find.

He picked it up. The feel of the cold steel, as he ran a finger along the serrated edge, was reassuring.

One, two, three steps and then he moved back into the hall. The glass once again scrunched underfoot. And, again, he was back in the porch. He was beginning to adjust – as much as anyone ever could – to being blind.

This time, however, there was no sound of chattery teeth, no sucking on the glass. *Maybe they've gone?* David thought. *Or maybe they've just moved away from the door to encourage me to come out?*

There was only one way to find out.

Before he'd gone to sleep, he had locked himself in, leaving the keys in the lock, as he always did.

He took a deep breath.

The keys jangled as he unlocked the door.

Pushing down the handle, he felt a cold breeze dapple his cheeks as he opened the door and stepped outside.

For a short while he just stood there, listening. Hoping that he wouldn't hear anything. Expecting at any moment for something to reach out and seize him, sink its razor-sharp teeth into him …

The short path ahead was lined with bushes. Making his way towards the main road, David used them for guidance, the knife held out in front of him. It was as he neared the pavement that he heard the chattering again – behind him.

Getting closer …

Moving out into the street, he stumbled over the curb and nearly fell. Trying to move as fast he could, whilst all the time wary of tripping over something and falling, he walked along the main road into town.

Every now and then his foot would hit the curb and he would have to adjust, try and find the centre of the road again. Abandoned cars were a problem, too. The nearer he got to town, the more he encountered. After twenty minutes, his legs and hips were bruised black and blue.

He heard a shotgun blast, followed by screaming, people calling for help, but there was nothing he could do. Trying to assist others would only delay him getting to Sandra; they would have to fend for themselves.

But it was the sound of the unseen enemy feasting on their victims that made David's skin crawl. There would be a pause, as if the creature were watching him as he fumbled past, temporarily interrupted while eating its bounty. Then, after he'd passed, he would hear the noises resume: the tearing, the ripping, the ravenous slavering.

And all the time he could hear that chattering.

Closing in.

Slowly closing in.

David pondered over why the creatures hadn't attacked him yet? *Maybe it's because of the knife?* he speculated. Quickly dismissing the idea when he remembered the gun-shots and the screaming. He wondered if they were just toying with him, tormenting him for a while before they …

No, he couldn't think about that. He had to keep his mind on the task ahead; he *had* to keep going.

But as the chattering sound grew steadily louder, ever closer, he thought about what had happened. How, all of sudden, the world had suddenly been plunged into a black abyss. How the creatures had turned up at *exactly* the same time. It was obviously no coincidence.

Shaking his head, he refused to speculate on the cause of the Blackout; he didn't need that mental torture on top of his fears for Sandra.

Soon, his world was reduced to the constant sounds of chattering, his plodding foot-steps, and the rasping whistle of his laboured breathing. He tightened his grip on the knife and forced himself onwards.

On the road that would take him to Sandra.

The creatures were in front of him now. They were behind him. They were all around him.

He kept walking …

The Head Gardener   Bruce Currie

This morning it was cold and it had been raining, and, apart from the dark one that was singing quietly to itself, its face white against the black soil, the heads were silent and bowed. They were planted in raised beds on three sides of the garden, at the base of bare, red brick walls streaked with damp. In and out of the shadows between them flickered light from the gardener's fire.

"Oo laa, loo laa," sang the head slowly, bending a little to the left on the first 'laa', then a little to the right on the second.

The gardener laid another bundle of wood on the fire and looked back at the house. The house, made of the same red brick, was small, rising not much higher than the walls. Its face was broken by two small windows, one directly above the other. His wife was standing at the lower window, looking up at the sky, watching the grey clouds chasing each other in the November wind. She was wearing the silencer already.

For a while, preoccupied by the washing up and the rushing clouds, she remained unaware of his gaze. Then something drew her eyes down and she caught sight of him looking in at her from the garden. She gave a shy smile and gestured to him to look away.

When he turned back to the fire, smiling, the sticks he had just laid there were blackening around the edges and little tongues of fire were flickering along their surface as they tried to gain a hold. He laid more wood into the fire and stood back, waiting for the fire to catch.

The singing head, warmed by the heat, made a sound like the purring of a cat, then began to improvise on the sound to create a new song that it hummed to itself contentedly. The gardener lowered his eyes and prodded the fire with a stick, making it crackle greedily as it drew the fresh wood in.

When the fire was ready he dropped the stick into it and picked up the silencer and the ropes. The ropes were tied together in an elaborate arrangement, one four foot length with three loops attached to it with slip knots at eighteen inch intervals. The ropes and the silencer would be his only protection.

As he walked over to the raised bed where the head was singing, the head moved too, its eyes following his movements with a dumb, curious look that he tried to avoid. He stopped in front of it and listened to the sounds for a moment – the singing, the crackle of his fire, wind gusting in trees beyond the wall – then it was all gone; the silencer was over his ears and all he could hear was the roaring of his own blood.

He clambered on to the raised bed. The head strained its neck to look up at him, but he didn't meet its eyes. He threw the loops of rope over the head, and stood behind it, feet planted firmly in the soil. He bent down, wrapped the crook of his elbow under its chin and placed his right hand at the nape of its neck. He could feel the jaw working – was it still singing?

He braced himself, shifting his feet slightly to balance his weight. The soil was wet and clumps of it stuck to the soles of his boots. He began to work the head out of the ground, twisting and pulling gently. The head shook itself desperately from side to side, but he held it firmly, little by little drawing it out until he could see the beginnings of thick roots, a bundle of pink, fleshy limbs, exposed between the neck and the black soil. With the tops of the roots free, he paused for a moment to rest, maintaining his firm grip between the throat and the nape of the neck. He needed to raise the head another six inches before he could secure the first of his three loops. He checked the position of the rope, then started to pull and twist the head to draw it further out. The more exposed the roots became, the more the head struggled, and the more difficult it was for him to hold it firm. When he'd made his six inches, he lifted the rope and tightened the first loop around the exposed bundle of roots. During this manoeuvre, the head, momentarily freed from his grasp, twisted around and spat at him. He caught the look of hatred in its eyes, and it was with dread that he returned to his task.

He drew the roots out another eighteen inches, then tightened the second loop. With the second loop tightened, his fear lessened a little and he pulled at the remaining roots more urgently, quickly raising the head to chest height and tightening the third loop. With all three loops in place he lifted the head entirely free of the soil and threw it to the ground where it thrashed impotently on the wet soil.

He stood above it for a moment, hands on hips, breathing heavily. For the first time he noticed that the other heads had lifted their faces and were swaying and mouthing something in concert. The swaying heads unsettled him and his sense of dread returned. Determined to get it over with as quickly as possible, he jumped down into the garden, turned, and lifted the uprooted head horizontally by the two outer loops. He carried it towards the fire, holding it at waist height, away from his body. It thrashed around vigorously like a large eel and it was all he could do to keep hold of it.

As he approached the fire he saw a movement out of the corner of his eye, from the direction of the house. He registered the movement but didn't react. All his attention was focused on getting rid of his burden, and with it his mounting fear.

He turned his back to the house to heave the head into the fire. The other heads stopped swaying and opened their mouths wide as he swung it back. He felt a prickling at the nape of his neck, but heard nothing. He started to fling the head, but before he could move, something grabbed him from behind and pinned his arms to his side. Unbelieving, he saw his wife's thin-fingered hands clasped across his chest. What was she doing? He tried to shake himself free, but while he held the head he could do nothing.

He dropped the head and prised apart his wife's hands. Still holding them apart he turned round to face her. She was shouting at him, silently, trying to free her hands so that she could hit him. Her face was distorted with an anger he'd never seen there before. To his horror he realized that she wasn't wearing the silencer – she could hear the heads!

He released her hands and pointed to his head, saying:

"Where is it?"

THE HEAD GARDENER   BRUCE CURRIE

But he heard neither his question nor her reply. She hit him several times on the arms and the chest and then started to pull at the silencer on his head. In a panic, he hit out and caught her a solid blow on the side of the jaw. Taken by surprise she stumbled backwards a few steps, lost her balance and fell over. Seizing the opportunity, he turned quickly, picked up the head and flung it on the fire. He watched only long enough to be sure the head was in the heart of the fire, then turned back to her. She was getting up from the floor quickly, looking at him as though he'd thrown a baby on the fire. She started to run towards the fire, but he intercepted her and started to drag her away. He had to get her back to the house, to put the silencer on.

She fought hard over every step and for all his strength he had difficulty holding on. At each step she dug her heels in and twisted and turned so that he had to keep renewing his grip, holding by the waist now, now precariously, with both hands holding one elbow. Step by step he drew her closer to the house. She broke from his grasp and he grabbed at her, flinging his arms around her upper body. In this desperate movement he left his right hand too close to her mouth and she fastened her teeth into it hard. Despite the pain he kept hold and started to pull her back. She bit harder, so hard that her teeth broke through the skin and muscle over his knuckles. With the sudden, sharp, excruciating pain, he let go, all his universe narrowed to the pain at the end of his arm. For a few seconds the only thing that mattered to him was his hand. While his wife ran towards the fire he drew the hand delicately to his chest, screaming silently with the pain. It was only when she stepped into the fire that he became aware of her again.

"No!"

As the hem of her dress burst into flames he dashed forward after her. She seemed impervious to the heat, reaching down into the flames to pick up the still squirming head as though reaching into a pool of water. He plunged into the flames after her and dragged her out, throwing her to the ground and rolling her in the soil to put out the flames. She fought him as he rolled her backwards and forwards, but he wasn't going to let her escape again. When the flames were out he forced her on to her belly and lay on her, using his weight to keep her from moving. For a long time, despite her position, she struggled against him. He could feel stinging burns on his legs and hands that grew steadily more painful, and with every movement she made, his broken knuckles shot a sharp pain up his arm.

Slowly her struggles quietened, the fight ebbing out of her. Even when she was still at last he continued to lie there. He felt his chest move up and down with the rhythm of her breathing. Her breaths became long and regular like the breaths of someone sleeping. For a moment, in this reverie, he felt something tender, almost sexual, in their position and he reached up to touch her hair. But the smell of sulphur and the feel of rough, charred ends brought him back.

Unable to use his right hand, with some difficulty he climbed off and sat beside her, nursing the hand to his chest. She lay still, naked apart from a few charred tatters of

cloth at her waist and shoulders. The sight of her skin, red where it wasn't black, sick-
ened him. The heads around the borders of the garden had lowered their faces again
and seemed sleeping too. In the fire nothing moved but the flames.

He sensed something behind him and turned. Where the dark head had been, where
there should now be a gap, there was a new head, blonde like the others. The face
seemed unfamiliar at first, draped in its loose blonde hair, looking around in bewilder-
ment, but when it turned full face to him, mouthing silently, he realised that it was his
wife's face. A tear began to form at the corner of its right eye, and it began to open its
mouth wider, trying to make him understand.

He looked around and saw that the other heads were raised now, all of them turned in
his direction. They were motionless, staring at him silently. He averted his eyes, looking
back at his wife. She too stared at him, tearful, mouthing silently. He looked up at the
sky, listened to the rush of his own blood, watched the clouds chasing each other across
the November sky. Then he reached up to take off the silencer.

Copyright © Bruce Currie 2011

Joe's Pet Store   Austin Hackney

You head into town to find Joe's Pet Store. Its easy enough. It sits right there on the main square. It's a big place with wide, light windows giving a good view of the interior even from the other side of the street. On sultry summer days, the door is propped open with a wedge of pinewood. And it doesn't smell bad like a lot of pet stores. It smells of fresh sawdust, sweet hay and good, dry grain. The animals they have in there – there's nothing exotic, just some fancy mice, piebald rats, a hamster or two, a flop-eared bunny, budgerigars, canaries, the usual stuff – all these are kept in almost clini-cally hygienic conditions: bright, beady eyes watch you from little bodies of glossy fur and well preened feathers. The budgies chunter and the canaries sing, carolling the scrag-bag pigeons that scrape the pavements outside, fattening themselves sick on shoe -crushed chips and dropped burgers smudged along the gutter. They told me that a cage door was carelessly left open once. Nobody noticed until the end of the day. But they found the bird was still sitting on its perch, flushed with health and happiness, as if it had all summer locked in its golden feathers. The canaries at Joe's know which side their bread is buttered on. What price freedom? They sing, taunting the grey pigeons' lot. Rats of the sky, they taunt from their gilded cages. Flying vermin.

You cross the street and step into Joe's. You're greeted by the two women who run the place: the older one, greying hair scraped back from her forehead and neatly pinned, sculptural age-lines lightly chiselled into good skin, alert green eyes; and the younger one, nut brown hair, glossy, tied into a loose ponytail, a stray lock breezing over a creamy complexion, green eyes like the older one, a glimpse of ivory teeth when she smiles.

These two women, mother and daughter you soon realise, are helpfulness and civility incarnate. There is nothing they will not do to accommodate your needs. And they will accompany you in person down the aisle to find just the right product for you and your little domesticated friend at home. They have everything you could possibly need or desire to keep your pet as healthy and happy as the exemplary models on display in the store. Yes, you can find anything at Joe's.

Apart from Joe.

He disappeared a while back.

Nobody knows why, how or where he went. No body was ever found.

But that's why you're here. To find out. The case was never closed and you have some new evidence that just might explain the mystery. Of course, you don't tell the ladies. Not yet. No point raising suspicions.

You are with the younger woman, admiring a cockatiel, whose crest rises slightly as you lean closer in towards the cage.

"He's embarrassed," you suggest, pointing a finger at the red blush of down on his cheeks.

"They're typical markings on this kind of parakeet," replies the woman, smiling.

"Ah yes," you reply. "Pretty things birds, but I'm more interested in small mammals;

gerbils, mice, rats, that sort of thing."

The young lady takes you lightly by the arm and leads you to the rats. There must be a dozen of them in three large cages. Most of them are sleeping, huddled together in a nest of straw. One is sniffing curiously. Its tiny, strangely human hands clutch at the shining bars. Its eyes are bright with visible intelligence. It is looking at you, assessing you, you think.

"Lovely creatures, aren't they?" croons the young woman.

You are getting closer to your moment. But you must be patient. Everything must lead on perfectly naturally.

"I've always liked them since I was a child," you lie, easily. "These are marvellous examples and in such fine condition. Still, I was hoping to find something more unusual. A rare colouration, for example, or a more distinctive marking."

"Well I'm sure we could find something for you. We have good contacts with the finest breeders."

The woman leads you back to the counter. She addresses her mother.

"The gentleman is interested in rare breeds. Could we find something for him?"

"That should be possible," answers the older lady. "I'll fetch the stock lists."

This is your chance. You take it.

"Do you have any other specimens, in the back maybe?"

You are sure the woman hesitates slightly. A momentary flicker of anxiety, quickly masked, in her green eyes.

"Everything for sale is in the shop."

"Everything for sale?" You leave the question hanging.

"We have our own pets, of course. Nothing that would interest a fancier such as yourself. I'll get the breeding lists. I won't be a moment."

And she disappears through the door behind the counter.

You turn to the younger woman.

"You keep rats?"

"Yes...well, we keep allsorts."

You notice that she has coloured slightly. You know she's lying. You know they keep only rats.

She's in your sights now. You shoot.

"Where's Joe?"

The woman pales. Her mouth opens and closes again.

"I'm sorry, I don't think..."

"What did you do with his body?"

You've studied the files. You know all about Joe: about his drinking, his violent behaviour, the lovers. The motives were always there. It was just that before there was so little evidence. You repeat the question. The woman is sliding behind the counter, backing towards the door.

"Who are you?" she says through dry lips.

"Criminal Investigation Department." You reach into your pocket and flash your ID.

"I don't know what you want. Dad disappeared…"

You go round the counter, push past her and through the door. Down a dimly lit hall-way, another door. The room is stuffy, over-furnished. There's a stale smell in the air. The older woman is reaching up to a shelf, to take down a box file. It has the words 'Stock Lists' printed on the cover. She spins round. She fumbles with the file and it falls to the ground, spilling papers on the plush carpet. She doesn't speak. She already knows who you are. She's guessing why you're here.

In the corner of the room is the cage of rats. Black rats, dozens of them. The sudden intrusion has agitated them and they squeak and crawl over one another, sniffing, scratching, twitching. They lift their heads and show long, yellowing incisors.

"I know what you did with Joe," you say. "A confession would make things easier."

"I don't know what you're talking about," she says. She's buying for time. She knows she's trapped. Than she becomes defiant. "You've no evidence."

"I've been doing some research. Rats are opportunistic feeders. If there's grain, the rat will eat it. If there's grain and an apple the rat will eat the grain first and then the apple. If there's grain, an apple and a steak the rat will eat some of the grain, some of the ap-ple and some of the steak. Take a black rat and starve it. Then put human flesh on the menu. The rat will eat that. If there's a starving colony they'll clean up: bones, hair, the lot."

The woman is shaking now, her voice quiet.

"You can't prove that," she says.

"We couldn't prove it," you say. "But then we found traces of rat droppings on your gloves. We ran DNA tests. Your rats had been eating strange pie. A confession would make things easier for you."

Suddenly she is defiant again.

"You'll never prove it!"

You sigh. Then you begin to pro-nounce the formula you have re-cited so often before.

"I am arresting you for the mur-der of your husband, Mr Joseph Hock. I must warn you that any-thing you say may be taken down and used in evidence…"

The woman is smiling. You hear the lock click in the door behind you. You turn round. The daughter is there. She has a baseball bat.

You reach for your revolver but she strikes first. You hit the ground hard. The pain in your skull is torment. You can taste blood. You open your eyes. The women are leaning over you. Their faces are intent, their breathing rapid. You can smell dental paste, breath freshener. It will be clean, hygienic. There will be no traces. The older one has a carving knife.

The last thing you see are the rats. Their starved bodies eager and frantic. Their eyes bright with hunger.

The Puddle   Richard Smith

We leave the house just before 7.00 am.

The sun has been up for a while. Rising over the distant hillside, its heat warms the chill dawn air, promising another hot summer's day.

Red pulls on the lead, eager to get into the woods. He's a good companion, an English Cocker Spaniel, four years old. He leaps and bounds without a care in the world.

The sky is a vivid blue. Birds sing from the trees. It could be an ordinary morning. Except today, the roads are quiet. There's no one else about. Right now, in homes across the country, and all over the world, people are sitting by their televisions and radios, waiting to hear the statement.

I already know what the news will be. I may have retired officially, but I still have good connections at the Observatory. An email came through from Mike Montgomery at 2.30 this morning. I couldn't sleep again after I read it.

Red isn't interested in the news. He's only interested in his usual morning routine. At quarter to seven this morning, as I sat in a tired, weary daze in the kitchen, I felt his nose nudging my hand.

"Come on then, old boy," I sighed, slipping on my shoes resignedly.

Red could not be happier as we reach the woods and I let him off the lead. He disappears into the cool shadows, and I follow. The fresh air is invigorating after the stale warmth of the house. Thoughts that were spinning in my head, competing for attention - recollections, treasured memories, missed opportunities, friends past and present; they settle now, a calm tranquillity descending as I walk.

I let Red decide where we will go today. He darts through the woods, emerging into the field beyond. I have to call him back to stop him getting too far ahead. He loops round, eyes watching me, tongue steaming, tail wagging. Then he curves off to the right, following the trail that leads down to the pond.

I follow, looking ahead, taking in the beauty of the valley before me. We've followed this same path so many times before. The grass is wild here, long and coarse. In places, brambles, honeysuckle, oak saplings and gorse encroach upon the path, attracting birds and wildlife.

As we descend I find myself thinking about the events that happened here, earlier in the year. I think of the news beaming out over the internet, the TV and radio, and I think of the tadpoles.

#

I remember when we first found them. It must have been early March. There had been heavy rain, and the path and surrounding grassland was flooded. Red bounded through the water, splashing happily. I strode after him in my Wellingtons. It was then that I saw the round bundles of jelly, clumped together, lying in the water - frogspawn.

Red made a cursory sniff, but was largely uninterested. I took a moment to look about. There were clumps of frogspawn everywhere. I could see no sign of actual frogs - they were no doubt nearby, but frogs are adept at hiding themselves.

The pond itself was still some way ahead, perhaps another quarter of a mile. The frogs had chosen this patch of watery ground to lay their spawn and I remember wondering how their tadpoles would fare - the flooding would soon recede and they would surely perish.

We came back that way on our morning walk most days the following week. The path continues down to the pond, and from there one can bear left, following another footpath that climbs back up to the village, a small circuit that takes about forty-five minutes.

There were other routes we could have taken, but I was interested in the frogspawn, and Red was content to splash through the wet grass. As it turned out, there was further rain that week, and the area remained flooded.

It was in the second week, when the wet weather became interspersed with sunnier, warmer spells, that the frogspawn broke down and dissolved. Wriggling like mad in the shallow water were thousands of tiny tadpoles. The water was ideal for them, crystal clear - so long as I was careful not to stir up the mud with my Wellingtons - and when the sun shone it sparkled and shimmered.

Throughout that week the water soaked slowly into the long grass on either side of the muddy trail. There was a deep depression in one place on the path which formed a puddle every time it rained, and in there the water remained, spanning the path, deep and wide.

The tadpoles, herded in by the gradually shrinking boundaries of the flooded area, gathered in the puddle in their thousands, their tiny bodies twisting and writhing, darkening the water with their numbers.

I found myself rooting for them, hoping they would survive. Each morning I watched, fascinated, observing them as they grew. I was struck by how fragile their existence was, their lives hanging by a thread, relying on the rain to sustain them.

As the days of March passed by, the rain became less frequent, the sun warmer. The winter cold receded, and the weather promised a warm Easter.

But despite the drier weather, against all odds, they continued to thrive. Whenever the puddle seemed about to dry up completely, there would be just enough rain overnight or during the day to replenish the water level and keep them going.

I was fascinated by that. It seemed reassuring, somehow.

#

I check the time. It's a quarter-past seven. I imagine families, crowded around TV screens, hearing the news, taking it in. People's lives have been on hold this last week.

The Crisis has affected everyone.

Events began when astronomers detected a long-period comet entering the outer reaches of the solar system. Its elliptical route took it close to the Sun, and as it streaked through the zone of the inner planets, it disturbed the orbital path of one particular chunk of rock, 1866-Sisyphus.

Sisyphus is an asteroid over eight kilometres in diameter, with a nickel-iron core, and its altered trajectory put it on a course dangerously close to the Earth.

Nobody could tell just how close, until the early hours of this morning. I've had five hours now to reflect on the prognosis.

I've known Monty for years. His curt email message was straight to the point. He advised that the latest set of observations put the probability of collision at 99.95%, as close to certainty as scientists will go.

"Within another day or two," the email read, "they will be able to predict the likely point of impact on the Earth's surface."

Not that it really matters, a rock that size.

I wonder how they are breaking the news to the world.

#

Few people walk along the trail here. The pond is not much to look at; it's overgrown and choked with weeds. Those who do use the path are generally dog walkers like myself. I usually see the same faces each morning. Most owners take their dogs out at a regular time.

I always say hello or good morning when I see someone. The funny thing is: I don't know any of the dog walkers' names. I know their dogs' names - Merlin, Mozart, Hudson, Rosie, Bracken - but not the owners'.

Hudson's owner is a widower. After his wife died, the dog is all he has left. A similar situation to me, I suppose. He's often out here with Hudson, taking several walks each day, and he always stops for a chat; always pleased to find someone to talk to.

One day, late in March, I was studying the tadpoles when Hudson's owner approached along the path. The puddle was no more than a few inches deep that day, just two or three feet across. The tadpoles did not seem to mind, though; they were much fatter and rounder, each body like a big, ripe raisin, the tails shorter, thick and strong.

Hudson reached me first, ignoring the puddle, his wet Labrador nose sniffing my pockets, searching for treats, finding none.

"Morning," I said as his owner arrived. He was a tall man, dressed in Wellingtons and raincoat like myself, although it was not raining that day. "I was just looking at these little fellows."

"Ah yes," he said, smiling. "They're getting bigger, aren't they?"

Red and Hudson began chasing each other, running and turning around in tight circles, and we watched them for a while.

"It's amazing how they manage to survive here. We seem to be getting just enough rain to keep them going. I keep expecting the puddle to dry, but they've been lucky so far."

Hudson's owner laughed. "I've been keeping an eye on them," he said. He pulled out a plastic water bottle from inside his coat. "Topping them up, each morning. Put a few biscuits in there every now and then, too. They seem to like them."

"Really?"

It seemed obvious then. I felt a little foolish. The rest of the ground there was quite dry. It should have occurred to me they were receiving help.

I shook my head ruefully. "I had no idea. I'd just put it down to nature's fine balance. Still, I guess we all need a little help sometimes - good for you."

After a while I whistled to Red and we continued on our way. I couldn't help smiling to myself as we walked on.

Following the news announcement this morning, the President of the United States is due to address the world. He will reveal the details of the joint American-Russian initiative, *Operation Spero* - the Latin word for hope.

The village church was full for the first time in memory last Sunday. I think it's human nature to look for hope in one form or another.

#

Red is bounding ahead, tail wagging, and I realise we've reached the spot where the tadpoles were, so many weeks before.

Their story is not quite finished. They had been growing nicely in the puddle, reaching the point where their bodies had taken on a distinct frog shape, their tails withdrawn, tiny legs visible. Their numbers had reduced, but those left, the strongest, the fittest, were flourishing.

Further rain had extended the size of their puddle, and with Hudson's owner also keeping an eye on their water level, not to mention feeding them surreptitious dog biscuits, their future seemed assured.

It was a sunny morning in early April when I discovered the puddle had been buried. I felt a physical jolt of alarm as my eyes stared at the mound of earth on the path. For a moment, I thought I was mistaken, that I was in the wrong place, but as I looked around there was no doubt.

This was the right place. The puddle had been filled in. Great shovelfuls of earth covered it completely. The mound rose to a level slightly higher than the rest of the path. The tadpoles had gone.

I spent the rest of that morning in a state of vague shock. I never did discover exactly what happened.

There was no sense to it. Who had filled it in? Why? What had happened to the tadpoles? I considered returning, digging up the earth, or perhaps calling the local Council, making some enquiries.

Then I felt I was over-reacting. In the end, I did nothing. I simply continued with my chores at home, pensive and slightly agitated.

I bumped into Hudson's owner the next morning.

The Puddle   Richard Smith

"Have you seen what's happened to the tadpoles?" I asked.

"Yes, funny, that," he replied.

"What happened? Who did it - do you know?"

"No idea. Just found it like that yesterday."

"I wonder if it was kids ..."

He shrugged. "I wouldn't have thought so. Why would they?"

"The Council then?"

"Could have been, I suppose. If someone complained about the path."

"What about the tadpoles, do you think they would have moved them first?"

He made a face; shrugged again. "I doubt it. It's just a few tadpoles, after all."

We went our separate ways. No doubt I was over-reacting. But I had enjoyed watching them grow - thriving, against the odds. The ending was so unexpected. It left me sad. It just felt so wrong. If the puddle had dried up, it wouldn't have been so bad. This was worse, somehow. And I was surprised by Hudson's owner. He didn't seem that bothered. Then again, like he said, it was just a few tadpoles. There are plenty more of them out there.

Life goes on.

I look up into clear blue sky.

#

In ancient Greek mythology, Sisyphus was a king. Punished by the Gods for his vanity and pride, he was forced to roll a huge boulder up a steep hill. Each time he reached the summit, the rock would roll back down to the base of the hill, and he would start again.

A meaningless and futile task; he was compelled to repeat it for eternity.

Monty's email contained one final piece of information. It concerned the joint American-Russian initiative. His department's independent calculations had shown the mission had almost no chance of success.

"Not a chance it will work," he had written. "They won't admit that, of course, but there's no way they could redirect their missiles in time. Then there's the question of physics. Even Newton could tell you an object of that size and velocity will not be perturbed by a few warheads. The very best that could happen is massive fragmentation, which could well increase the hazard. It's hopeless, old boy."

Tonight, I'll come back out with Red and look at the stars.

I've spent my whole life looking at them; it's an interest I've held since I was a child. On a clear night, from the top of the valley you can see the heavens from horizon to horizon.

There are literally billions of stars out there in our galaxy, and billions more galaxies like our own. The numbers are quite staggering - I find it humbling when I consider it; it's hard to even comprehend.

Red looks at me expectantly as we reach the junction in the path. I nod for him to take the track back up to the village.

There's nothing to be done. All we can do is go back to our house, and wait.

MIRA   IAIN PATON

I
Kagame
鏡

It happened a long time ago, during the era of the Tokugawa Shogunate. The village of Hirawara was five days ride from Edo, surrounded by fertile rice fields beside the Ara-kawa river. The long-beloved daimyo Yoshimuro Hirawara had recently died. His only son and heir Ieyasu had assumed rule of the province, although he was suspected by some of hastening his father's untimely death. Ieyasu was a bad son, self-indulgent and prone to violence. However, no one realised what a bad ruler he would turn out to be.

During the spring of that year, as the cherry blossoms were flowering, Ieyasu issued a decree which shocked even those who knew him. It was short and to the point.

More bushels of rice were to be paid to Edo in taxes.
There was no place for unproductive peasants, the elderly, or the sick.
One such peasant would be selected for weekly samurai sword practice.

The passing of one month had seen the killing of four peasants – an old man, an old woman, an idiot man and a lame beggar; all slaughtered at sunrise. It was rumoured that Ieyasu would be greatly amused by the murder of a child split in two with a single strike of the sword. This could not go on, and so, on the evening following the slaughter of the beggar, the village elders held a conference in the sake house of the village.

The discussion did not last long before the door slid open. A samurai strode in. Those nearby bowed in obedience, but the elders were too shocked to do anything but stare in fear. The samurai sat down on an unoccupied stool at their table, taking his swords from his kimono belt and placing them on the table. The elders relaxed slightly, as they recog-nised the samurai. Hideyaki had been the most trusted retainer of the previous daimyo and it was rumoured he had fallen out of Ieyasu's favour. He was known as a wise and humane man.

"I know what you are plotting," said Hideyaki, "and there is very little that can be done." He gestured for a flask of sake and refilled the cups.

"We can't launch a surprise attack in force, as we don't have enough men to follow our banner," explained Hideyaki. "Ieyasu has bought many men whose souls worship only gold."

He leaned back on the stool and drained his cup of sake in a single gulp.

"It is impossible to raise an army and lay siege to the castle," he sighed. "It would take too long and Edo would intervene when the flow of taxes stopped."

Hideyaki's cup was refilled by one of the elders.

"We can't employ an assassin as Ieyasu has surrounded himself with guards and the assassin would be caught,' he said. "His revenge on the village would be terrible."

Again, the samurai drank the cup of sake in a single swallow. He leaned forward.

"However, there is one plan that might work." He held up his hand and a man walked forward from the shadows.

If the elders had been afraid before, they were now terrified. The man was Obuko, a well known monk. He lived in the hills to the north of the village, and was rarely seen. It was said that he had killed a man simply by staring at him and that he communicated with the demons of Hell. Obuko's shaved head gleamed as he sat down.

The monk explained. There was a way to get rid of Ieyasu, he said, but it would cost a thousand koku. This would not be for his own personal benefit, as he had no need of material possessions, but would be required to purchase certain items. The sum was large, very large, and would nearly break the village. Obuko stood up abruptly and said he needed the money, whether in coins or in items of value, by sunset of the next day, in order to make his preparations.

Hideyaki watched as the monk left, before speaking softly.

"You heard Obuko," he said. "There is a way, but it will cost a great deal."

He pushed the swords across the table to the village elders.

"These are yours now. They will fetch a good price, but you will need to work hard to find the rest. You know where to send word to me." The samurai stood up and left.

The elders worked quickly. By sunset the next day they had raised the necessary sum in gold and in valuables. The pawnbrokers of Edo would be kept busy. The elders watched as a small cart was loaded with their valuables, before it trundled off into the hills.

Nothing happened the next day, the second day since the murder. The elders watched and waited. Nothing happened the following day, either.

II
Mira
ミラー

Yoshio was bored. The classroom was hot and humid, and the air conditioning system was struggling to cope with the Yokohama summer. The lesson was science and he was looking forward to the lunchtime *bento* box of rice and pickles followed by a short break in the schoolyard swopping *manga* books. They had English class after lunch, with the gangly American exchange teacher. They laughed at him behind his back, but in a kindly way.

"Pay attention, Yoshio," his teacher barked.

Twenty-nine faces turned to look at him. Ashamed, he slouched down behind his desk. The classroom monitor passed around the textbooks, for home study.

"The science lesson next week will be on light," the teacher said, writing on the board.

Yoshio idly opened the textbook, flicking through the pages and glancing at the diagrams showing beams of light bending in various directions. He saw something briefly, a folded piece of paper, as the pages fluttered by. He flicked backwards but couldn't see it, and flicked forwards again. There it was, towards the back. He pulled it out. *Maybe a love note or a suicide note*, he thought. He glanced around to make sure no-one was watching, and opened it. There was a scrawled message inside. He decided to read it later.

Yoshio read the note in the toilet. He sat on the western-style toilet with the lid down and his trousers on. He opened the note. There was a scrawled message.

The *kanji* for mirror, or *kagame,* caught his eye instantly.

鏡

Intrigued, he read the note. It was a haiku.

鏡

A pair of mirrors
Face each other at sunset
Three nights, shadow nears

He folded the note up and put it in his pocket. Lessons would be starting again shortly.

Yoshio forgot about the note that afternoon as his friends were planning a weekend trip to Shinjuku, the fashion district of Tokyo. His family holiday was also getting closer and Yoshio was looking forward to the week away at the beaches of Enoshima. It would be just him, his mother and father, and the family would enjoy a break from the hectic pace of life. At home, school nights were usually rushed, and he would slurp down curry and noodles at the kitchen breakfast bar of their small flat before watching some TV and then going to bed.

He was undressing for bed when he felt the square of notepaper through the trouser pocket. He brought out the note and read it again.

鏡

A pair of mirrors
Face each other at sunset
Three nights, shadow nears

Yoshio put on his pyjamas and padded into his parents' room. There was a full-length mirror bordered in red-black lacquer. There was also a similar mirror in the hall. Both were hung from wall hooks and could be removed and replaced easily. He tiptoed across to the mirror before stopping. It was nearly dark and his parents would soon be getting ready for bed themselves. His mother worked as an administrator and his father was a recently-appointed junior executive, proud that he had moved on from being a salary-man. They worked long hours, and were often out when Yoshio returned. There would be another chance, another sunset. He went to bed, looking forward to the coming weekend.

III

Kagame

鏡

The next day, late in the afternoon, a wagon was seen approaching the castle. What happened next was pieced together later on from whispered rumours.

The cart had delivered two giant silvered mirrors. These were a gift from Edo, and de-signed to be mounted on walls facing each other in a throne room or audience hall. They created the illusion of eternal space stretching out on either side, a sense of great-ness. Ieyasu had received the mirrors with childlike delight, and they were mounted in his throne room within an hour. He gave instructions for a lavish gift to be sent to Edo in return, before settling to watch the lamplight flickering in the mirrors; diminishing rows of light stretching into infinity on either side. Shortly after sunset that night, Ieyasu had called for his guards. He thought he had glimpsed something skulking in the shadows. It was surely an assassin, and he would not have been alerted were it not for the mirrors. The guards searched the throne room and moved outwards to search throughout the entire castle. They found no intruder, no assassin. Ieyasu retired to his bedchamber, reassured.

The following day dawned on a fearful village. The peasants and tradesmen had sacri-ficed almost all their possessions to be rid of Ieyasu, but nothing had happened. His sol-diers were knocking on doors, inquiring after the health of children. It would not be long before one was taken to the castle. Once more, rumours spoke of what had happened at the castle that night.

Ieyasu had called for his guards in panic. He had seen a masked figure dressed all in black. There was no doubt, he had definitely seen an assassin. The figure had darted from one side of the room to the next, caught in the reflections of the mirrors. Once again, there was a search, and nothing was found. Ieyasu decided he would not leave the throne room, and he had his futon moved from his bedchamber and laid out in the throne room by his servants.

The next day, the day before sword practice, Ieyasu's soldiers were kept busy. They were searching for an assassin and they were searching for a victim. A child was found, a little girl. The village held its breath and waited. The elders knew they had placed all their hopes on the monk's plot, so they waited in fear. The unfortunate child was taken to the castle and imprisoned until dawn the following day, the morning of the sword practice.

IV
Mira
ミラー

Yoshio loved the waterfront of Yokohama. He had missed the trip to Shinjuku with his classmates. He had tried to get the wrong train, or it had been cancelled, or something. He wasn't quite sure. He knew they called him *otaku,* or nerd, behind his back. This used to bother him, but not so much now. He loved the *Train Man* manga comic, *Densha Otoko*, about the nerd who rescues a woman on a train. He was happy as he strolled along the waterfront gardens, the Landmark Tower and sail-like buildings curving down to the harbour in the distance. *You can see Mount Fuji from the Landmark Tower*, he thought, *and the lift is really fast*. He decided to buy a steamed pork bun and work out his plan for the mirror experiment.

Yoshio had read the science book from cover to cover in bed the previous night, to glean as much information as possible. He had read about experiments and how to conduct them. He had researched the sunset time, just after 7pm. That was perfect as his mother would be watching television and his father would be playing *mah-jongg* with his work colleagues. His mother never moved from the television on a Saturday night. He would run the experiment later. He would also keep a notebook, an experiment log, with dates and times and descriptions of all that happened.

Before heading home, Yoshio visited the pachinko arcade to play the children's machines, which offered small toys rather than cash prizes. He had paid little attention as the small steel balls whirled around the machine. He left empty-handed and made his way to the subway for the journey home.

"Hello, Yoshi-chen," his mother called as he entered the flat. Yoshio kicked off his shoes and pulled on his slippers before heading into the kitchen. His noodles were in a plastic container, ready to be microwaved, with sauce in a small pan on the cooker. Yoshio wolfed down his noodles in front of the TV, his eye on the clock. *6pm.* He showed his mother the textbook and explained he was doing an experiment for school. His mother was not particularly interested, but she was enthusiastic that he was taking an interest in his lessons and offered to help. She helped him take the mirrors down from the wall. He dragged the mirrors into his room. He put one mirror against his bed and propped the other mirror against a chair, moving them so they faced each other. He took out his notebook and turned to the first page. *Experiment Log*, he wrote in bold characters. He copied the haiku on to the first page, and stapled the original note to the inside front cover for good measure. He read it again.

鏡

A pair of mirrors

Face each other at sunset
Three nights, shadow nears

Yoshio checked his watch. *6.35pm*. He wasn't sure what to do, so he stuck his head in between them. He looked left, into a wide mirror-tunnel stretching into infinity. He could see his face looking back at him, the surrounding mirror frame reflected time and time again, a winding and twisted ladder which curved upwards and out of sight. He felt dizzy, as if he was being sucked into the world beyond the glass. He turned and looked to his right. The view was the same. A mirror corridor curving into eternity.

Yoshio pulled back with a shudder of vertigo. He checked his watch. Seven minutes until sunset.

Yoshio noted in his log. *6.53pm. Nothing observed.*

He sat back and re-read the note, trying to understand what to look for. It now occurred to him that the haiku may be an obscure code, not referring to a clear phenomenon.

Yoshio returned to his position between the mirrors. He looked up the mirror-tunnels into the infinite distance, choosing the left-hand mirror to search with screwed-up eyes. His watch beeped. *7.00pm*. It was just before sunset.

There, in the distance -
A glimpse of fleeting shadow
Distant flash of black.

Just for a moment, before it vanished.

Yoshio looked again, staring deep into the mirror curve, before crawling backwards from between the mirrors.

What was it? he thought in shock.

His hand shook as he scribbled in the log. *A Shadow, far away.*

He was scared, but exhilarated. He put his experiment log on his bedside table and propped the mirrors up against the wall, so he would be able to roll out his futon at bedtime.

On Sunday, Yoshio was left alone at home, as his mother visited her relatives. His father was at the baseball game, with his work colleagues. It was overcast outdoors, so he played video games for most of the day. The day passed slowly, painfully slowly, as he was eager to repeat the experiment.

Eventually the sun sunk towards the horizon, and the time came for the second experiment. Yoshio had not yet replaced the mirrors on the walls. He put his head between the mirrors. He heard a beep. *7.00pm*. It was just before sunset. He screwed up his eyes and looked up and down, left and right.

A shadowy shape,

Like a human silhouette -
It is closer now

It was getting closer.
Yoshio wrote in his logbook. *Black Shadow Man. Getting closer. Half way now.*
He moved the mirrors apart and propped them up against the wall. He had a flash of inspiration. He would borrow the video camera and record the next experiment.

V
Obuko
お武庫

The monk sits on the tatami flooring of his small mountainside house. The paper walls glow with the orange rays of the setting sun, which is framed in the open doorway. He looks to his right and left, at the tarnished mirrors which he sits between. The mirrors had been made to order by the mirror-maker Hokusai in Edo, some time ago.
It is time.
The monk reaches for his ink-pot and parchment. He scribes carefully, without looking at the parchment, as he crafts the *kanji* characters.

A pair of mirrors
Face each other at sunset
Three nights, shadow nears

The *kanji* for mirror, kagame – 鏡

The *kanji* for shadow, kage – 影

There, in the distance –
A glimpse of fleeting shadow
Distant flash of black

The monk rests his brush. He looks at what he has written. The sun has set now and only the small lantern hanging from the ceiling casts any light. He blows lightly to extinguish the flame of the oil lamp and lies down on his futon. He closes his eyes.
The next evening, at sunset, he watches the path of the descending sun once more. Its light turns the waters of the Arakawa River into molten gold. Once more, it sinks behind the distant horizon.
It is time.
The only sound is the monk's soft breathing and the scraping of the brush on parchment.

A shadowy shape,
Like a human silhouette
It is closer now

The monk looks at what he has written. He blows softly to extinguish the flame of the oil lamp and lies down upon his futon. He closes his eyes.

The final evening, at sunset, he watches the sun sink again. The sky is a sea of small clouds, ships of purple and orange, and he watches as the sun sinks beneath them. It is time.

The brush scrapes the paper.

There, even closer –
A shadow man with no face
Close enough to touch

Suddenly, he darts across to each mirror in a flash, turning them face down. He exhales slowly, a sigh of relief. He removes the necklace from his neck, a glinting shard of mirror. The charm has worked. He looks at the parchment, reading the verses. A drop of ink has fallen from the brush onto the paper beneath the verses. He is not sure if it has spoiled or enhanced the calligraphy. Perhaps it is *wabi sabi*, the beauty of imperfection. He looks back at the mirrors, which he had turned before the pregnant drop had even hit the page. He will not repeat the ritual again, it is too dangerous and he has seen enough. He blows gently to extinguish the flame of the oil lamp and lies down upon his futon. He closes his eyes.

VI

Mira

ミラー

Monday was school day. Yoshio heard his schoolfriends discussing their shopping trip to Shinjuku. Apparently the trip had not been cancelled, or they had all managed to get another train, or something. He was used to it.

Yoshio was well-prepared for the science lesson that morning, even answering a question asked by the teacher. He did not mention the experiment to anyone. At lunchtime he retreated to the toilets and stared into the polished steel mirror above the washhand basins. He saw his face reflected, unremarkable except for a small mole on his left cheek. His mirror-face had a mole on its right cheek. He looked around for any sign of a shadow-creature. There was no sign. Two mirrors were clearly required, at the appropriate time. Yoshio's mirror meditations were interrupted by the clattering of the toilet door as it swung open. He quietly went about his business, washing and drying his hands as his schoolmates darted noisily about him.

The afternoon dragged on, heavy with anticipation. Yoshio fell foul of the teacher as his attention drifted in class. He had been caught staring out of the window, or rather *at* the window, gazing at his glazed reflection until the spell was shattered by the inevitable admonishment. Eventually, much later, it was time to go home.

He was eager to get home, and ran some of the distance, his school-bag swinging behind him. The routine was predictable as always, slurping down noodles in the kitchen with his mother, before she watched TV. His father would not be home until much later, so he had plenty of time. Of course, it was only the time of sunset that mattered.

That evening, Yoshio set up the mirrors again. He placed the video camera at an angle and checked the viewfinder. He could see part of the left-hand mirror through the camera.

He checked his watch. *6.40pm.* Sunset was nineteen minutes away. He fidgeted, rearranging his experiment log and checking the camera again. Shortly before the appointed time, he switched on the camera, checked his watch again and crawled between the mirrors, both boy and camera staring into the mirror abyss. His watched beeped. *6.58pm.* Just before sunset.

Later on that night, Yoshio's mother Noriko checked the wall-clock. *9pm.* She got up from the sofa. *What is that boy doing*, she wondered. It was school tomorrow and he needed to get to bed. Noriko walked to Yoshi's bedroom. She knocked on the door.

"Time for bed, Yoshi-chen," she called. There was no answer.

She opened the door, peering round it. The room was dark. *He must be asleep already*, she thought. Rather than disturb him, she closed the door and tiptoed to the kitchen. He had looked tired earlier, anyway. Noriko put a bottle of beer in the fridge for her husband, for his return from work, and returned to the sofa.

VII
Kagame

Finally, the day of sword practice dawned. It seemed that nothing had happened and the poor girl was doomed to die with the rising sun. However, the alarm was raised shortly before dawn. Ieyasu's guards had gone to wake him, as he had requested, so he could attend the sword practice. They found nothing. Ieyasu was not there. The castle was searched and he was not found. The village was searched and he was not found. Someone thought they had seen a fleeting shadow the previous night, but it was probably a flicker of torchlight. In any case, there was no body, so it could not have been an assassination. Ieyasu was gone.

Later that morning, Hideyaki walked up the road to the castle, unarmed. He spoke with the guards before passing through the gate. The girl was released, and by noon that day, Hideyaki had assumed the lordship of Hirawara. By this time, rumours of the previous events had spread throughout the village.

Not long afterwards, the monk Obuku was found dead. He was discovered on the road southwards from the village, dressed and equipped for a long journey. The villagers had searched his shack, in the hills to the north of the village, in the belief that their wealth was hidden there. Very little was found, except for a parchment upon which was written a series of haiku verses -

鏡

A pair of mirrors
Face each other at sunset
Three nights, shadow nears

There, in the distance –
A glimpse of fleeting shadow
Distant flash of black

A shadowy shape,
Like a human silhouette
It is closer now

There, even closer –
A shadow man with no face
Close enough to touch

One of the elders recalled a myth of a mirror-demon, a shadow creature which would appear in a mirror at sunset. If there was a person nearby at this time, caught between two mirrors, it would pull the person's soul into the mirror-world. The shadow creature would then escape into the mortal world – an exchange of a soul for a soul.

Not long afterwards, the elders found out that Hideyaki had given two orders immediately after his assumption of authority. The first was the release of the girl. The second was the removal of the mirrors from the throne room, which were melted down and used to fund improvements in the village. Whatever truth lay behind Iesayu's disappearance, the elders were certain it had been worth every koku.

VIII
Kage

6am. The alarm clock beeped. Noriko heard her husband get up and leave for work, but she managed to sleep until 7am when the alarm beeped again. She padded through to the kitchen to make Yoshio's breakfast, and a cup of coffee for herself.

There was no sign of her son.

Noriko knocked on his bedroom door. No answer. She opened the door.

Yoshio's futon was rolled up and he was not in the room. Just those two mirrors, propped up facing each other, an exercise book on the floor and the video camera between the mirrors. The curtains were open and daylight streamed in.

Noriko darted out to the lobby. Yoshio's shoes were still there. He had not left the flat. She checked the kitchen again, the living-room and the bathroom, with spiralling anxiety. No Yoshio.

Heart pounding, she went back to his bedroom. She checked the wardrobe and behind the curtains. No Yoshio. She felt a surge of panic. She saw the exercise book and picked it up. *Experiment Log*. She opened it.

鏡

A pair of mirrors
Face each other at sunset
Three nights, shadow nears

Day 1. 6.53pm. Nothing observed. 7.01pm. A Shadow, far away.
Day 2. 6.59pm. Black Shadow Man. Getting closer. Half way now.
Day 3. 6.58pm.

Noriko grabbed the camera and ran through to the living-room, plugging the camera in with shaking hands, fumbling with the cables. She rewound the tape. It took an eternity to reach the beginning. She pressed *play*.

The screen is blue at first. There is a mirror at an angle. It faces another mirror, and they are reflecting each other. Yoshio's head appears between the mirrors. He looks at the camera and smiles, he is excited. He turns his head to his left. His reflected face is visible. The small mole on his left cheek is on the right cheek of his mirror-face. He is looking at something beyond the viewpoint of the camera. His mirror-face eyes widen in excitement, and then in fear. His mouth opens, a silent gasp of horror. There is a flash of blackness and a shadow passes in front of the camera. The shadow is gone. So is Yoshio. The mirror is still there. The picture gradually darkens as the sun sets and the tape ends just before the room is completely dark.

She reached forward and pressed the rewind button, her heart pounding. She replayed the tape again, in slow motion this time.

His reflected face is visible. The small mole on his left cheek is on the right cheek of his mirror-face. He is looking at something beyond the viewpoint of the camera. His mirror-face eyes widen in excitement, and then in fear. His mouth opens, a silent gasp of horror. There is a flash of blackness and a shadow passes in front of the camera.

Wait – something wasn't right –
She paused the tape, rewinding it before replaying that particular section frame by frame.

His reflected face is visible. The small mole on his left cheek is on the right cheek of his mirror-face. He is looking at something beyond the viewpoint of the camera. His mirror-face eyes are wide in excitement, and in fear. His mouth is open, a silent gasp of horror.

Forward a frame – there it is –

His reflected face is visible. The small mole on his left cheek is on the left cheek of his mirror-face. He is looking at something beyond the viewpoint of the camera. His mirror-face eyes are wide in excitement, and in fear. His mouth is open, a silent gasp of horror. His mouth gapes like a landed fish, looking out from a mirror-world as he is sucked into its depths, in an instant.

Noriko screamed. She grabbed the camera and ran into Yoshio's room to get the notebook. The door slammed behind her as she ran barefoot down the stairs, out of the apartment block and into the busy street. The police station was across the road, a short distance away.
She hadn't noticed the shadow. It had followed her, flitting furtively from darkness to blackness. It hung back now, in the shade of a doorway, and waited before pouncing.
The bus hit Noriko as she darted out into the road. It knocked her off her feet and her head smacked wetly against the tarmac. Some children screamed.
She hadn't stood a chance, agreed the policemen, as her body was zipped up into a black plastic bag. Something must have distracted her and stopped her seeing the bus. Witnesses said that she had appeared distressed and in a rush. She had been carrying something but no one had found anything at the scene. Some children, maybe young teenagers, had seen the accident but they had vanished.

* * * * * * * * * * *

The following night, in a Tokyo apartment, a young girl sat down in front of her computer. Mariko had homework to do, but first she checked her email. There was a message from her friend, entitled *Mira – freaky!* The email had a video file attached.

MIRA   IAIN PATON

鏡

A pair of mirrors
Face each other at sunset
Three nights, shadow nears

Day 1. 6.53pm. Nothing observed. 7.01pm. A Shadow, far away.
Day 2. 6.59pm. Black Shadow Man. Getting closer. Half way now.
Day 3. 6.58pm.

Mariko had twenty-seven friends in her address book. She watched the video clip and forwarded the email to them all. They would forward it in turn. The next evening, a hundred mirrors would be taken down before sunset, more again the following night.

Copyright © Iain Paton 2011

THE PAPER GARDEN   SALLY QUILFORD

Rav was just about to go to lunch when the alarm sounded. A message flashed up on his screen relating to Prisoner 24509. Rav tapped another part of the screen, which opened up a channel in his earpiece.

"Miss Sullivan, could you come to the Control Room, please?"

Five minutes later, she arrived, her high heels clacking on the cold stone floor. The sound made Rav shiver. Not an unpleasant feeling around Anne Sullivan.

"Prisoner 24509 has committed suicide," Rav told her.

"What? Are you sure?" Anne looked at the screen, but she needed Rav to explain it to her. A black computer screen overlaid with green lines forming a grid held the word *Wilderness* in the centre. "There's nothing there that he could harm himself with. He might have just died."

"No, we'd have had some warning of his vitals shutting down. According to the read out from his monitor, he just decided to switch off. It's odd. He's been out there for ten years. Usually people die of the despair long before that."

"Get the team to pick up his body and take it back to his family." Anne tapped the console with long fingernails.

"You seem angry, Anne."

"Do I? Why should I be? We drop criminals in the Wilderness and leave them to their own devices. According to the Great Nation it's the most humane death sentence ever developed."

The metal door whirred shut behind Kitty, leaving her alone in the cell. Dank steel walls closed in on her, even though she had more room to move than she'd ever had at home on the Reservation, sharing with her husband and two children.

She'd been given a few sheets of paper explaining the prison rules. Kitty sat on the bed and tried to read them. She made out her own name, tracing it with her fingers. The rest were abstract symbols that hid the mysteries of the world from her. No one had bothered asking if she could read, and she was too shy to say. She did the only thing she knew what to do with paper; what her father had taught her many years before. She styled the first sheet into a rose and the second into a bird, and placed them on the floor in the corner of the cell, opposite the stinking commode. A paper garden in a sea of steel.

That night, she lay awake listening to the sounds around. Women sobbing, others railing against the system and the evil men who'd put them there; still more making sounds that Kitty recognised, but didn't believe could be happening. Not among women with no men.

The following day, when Mags caught Kitty in the washroom – as the female warder dealt with a problem elsewhere - she was taught to believe how those sounds might happen. Not that Kitty dared make a sound as Mags hands searched out her secrets and coerced Kitty into learning hers. She tried to retreat into the world she had created as a child, but the harsh reality of her situation rendered her unable to escape, even into her dream world. By the end of the quick, brutal assault, Mags ragged fingernails had left their mark on Kitty's body.

"You'll be my little friend from now until you go to the Wilderness," Mags told her. Kitty nodded, afraid of what Mags might do if she refused.

"Do you need anything?" Anne asked Kitty, when she visited her a few days later. Kitty was tempted to reply that she'd like some respite from Mags, but she shook her head. The prison psychologist was smarter than Kitty gave her credit for. "Did you read the rules, Kitty? About how no one must engage in sexual activity?"

The warder who'd failed to keep watch in the washroom was standing near the door, so Kitty said nothing of Mags. "I can't read very well," said Kitty.

"Oh, I see. I'm sorry, Kitty, no one told me. Where are the papers I gave you?"

Kitty nodded towards the corner, where her paper garden was taking shape. She was sure she'd get a beating now.

"You do origami!" said Miss Sullivan.

"No," said Kitty, convinced she'd just been accused of some heinous crime, and suspecting it might have something to do with Mags. "I just make stuff with paper."

Miss Sullivan smiled, but she looked sad. "I'll get you some paper so you can make more flowers. Would you like that?"

"Yes, thank you."

"But you need to keep one of those papers safe. The one that you've made into a bird is an important document about ..." Miss Sullivan stopped, as if the rest were too embarrassing to say. "It's about the Wilderness, Kitty."

"When will I go there?"

"We don't have a date yet, but your lawyer is appealing."

"I don't have a lawyer, Miss Sullivan."

"Yes, you do. The court appointed one for you."

"He didn't like me so I don't think he'll be trying too hard."

"He'll be expected to do his job, Kitty."

When Kitty failed her appeal a week later, she was relieved. The Wilderness had to be better than Mags' constant attentions.

"You leave in the morning, Kitty," Anne Sullivan told her. "I have to warn you that there can be no escape from the Wilderness. You'll be fitted with a chip so that we can monitor you, and you'll be sent right back there if you do try to get out."

"I won't try to escape."

"I see your garden is growing," Miss Sullivan said, looking into the corner. A leafy shrub and a sunflower had joined the rose and bird. Several smaller flowers, which Miss Sullivan couldn't name, appeared to be growing out of the walls. "I'm afraid there'll be no paper where you're going, and you can't take those with you. Is there anyone you'd like me to send them to? Your parents?"

"No. They don't speak to me now. Not since …"

"I wanted to ask you about that, Kitty. You've been an exemplary prisoner, and I know you've had trouble with Mags, without retaliating. You're so gentle, in fact, that I can't understand why you killed your children."

"It was better for them to be away from it."

"Away from what, Kitty?"

"From their father's violence."

"Why didn't you leave?"

"He was my husband." Kitty held out her wrist to show the brand: two rings entwined burned into her skin, crisscrossing pale blue veins.

"I know branded marriages still go on in some cultures," said Miss Sullivan, "but as far as the Great Nation is concerned, they're not legally binding. I mean that you didn't have to stay, Kitty."

Kitty faltered. That's not what Frank told her. He always said that if she left him, she'd be arrested for breaking their contract. He'd wave the piece of paper in front of her face, knowing she couldn't read it.

"Miss Sullivan," said Kitty, just as Miss Sullivan was about to leave her.

"What is it, Kitty?"

"Is Mags going to the Wilderness too?"

"No. Mags is serving a lighter sentence and will be set free soon. She won't bother you again, Kitty."

"Thank you, Miss. You've been very kind to me. You can have my paper garden when I've gone - if you want."

"Kitty," said Anne. "Is there anything you'd like to tell me before you go? About your children?"

"I'm very sorry for what I did. I deserve to be punished."

"Is that the truth?"

"Yes, I'm sorry."

"No, I mean about what you did to your children."

"Yes. It was me. I said so, didn't I?"

Later that day, when Kitty went to the showers, a guard stayed with her, and remained with her throughout the evening meal and leisure hour. All Mags could do was glower in frustration.

Anne Sullivan entered the control room, way down in the basement of the prison, and took a seat next to Rav. Somehow he never needed other lights, taking all the illumination he needed from the bank of computer screens. Whilst Anne was tempted to turn the lights on, she knew better than to interrupt Rav's train of thought. He could keep tabs on every prisoner in the Wilderness and still find time for a game of online Scrabble.

"Where is she now?" asked Anne.

"She'll be dropped off in a moment. There she is look." Rav pointed to a shadow on the screen. "Keep your eye on that. It's moving fast at the moment, because she's in the chopper. It'll slow down when she gets out."

"I can't help thinking we've made a mistake with her," said Anne.

"You mean she didn't take an axe to her two children? On what do you base that, Anne? Because she makes pretty figures out of paper?"

"Yes. Sort of. She just didn't seem the type. God knows we've had some hard women in here, and some who were good at pretending to be helpless. But Kitty bothers me. She's too docile. If she had all that anger in her, why didn't she use it against Mags?"

"Some people only commit one crime in their life. But when they do, it's usually a big one. Here, she's landed." Rav pointed to the screen, where the blip rested between the e and r of *Wilderness*. "I'll watch her for a couple of days, then set the computer to alert me if she moves outside the boundaries."

"Assuming she survives."

Kitty enjoyed the helicopter ride. She could see all of the Great Nation below her, including the edge of the Reservation. The chopper headed north, and landed in the middle of a desert.

"This is it," said the pilot. "Out you get, Kitty."

She hesitated before following orders. As it left her, the chopper threw up a blanket of sand. Kitty covered her face until it settled back onto the ground.

Eventually it cleared enough for her to look around. The Wilderness lay before her, a vast space full of nothingness. She'd expected other prisoners to be there. Maybe they'd gone further across the desert, she mused, but looking out into the distance, she saw only sand and, nearer to her, a solitary rock. She didn't know it, but it marked the exact centre of the Wilderness.

The longer she stared at the sand, the stranger it seemed, as if it were an ocean, ebbing and swaying, towards her, then away, to the left, to the right. The ground under her feet felt steady enough, albeit like a sandpit, but the whole scene appeared to move before her eyes.

The sun beat down on her and the thick woollen dress she wore soon became damp and itchy. Her tongue was already starting to feel dry. She wondered how she'd manage to eat or drink, as there was nothing around. Just as she thought it, she turned and saw a bottle of water. It was half covered in sand, which was why she hadn't seen it earlier. How it would be replenished, she didn't know.

Ignoring the bottle, despite her growing thirst, Kitty sunk to the ground, pulling her knees up to her chest, searching for some inner equilibrium. It was a thing she used to do as a child, and what her father called 'Kitty's coma', when she'd switch off everything around her and retreat into a world over which she had complete control, building worlds where she was queen.

When she married, Frank had taken to knocking her out of her self-made kingdom, to the point that she dare not go there again. She soon realised there would be no escape from him, but she found a good facsimile of it, all too briefly, in her children. After all, mothers were supposed to buy into their children's fantasies. Frank, jealous of the time she spent with them, took that away from her.

The day – Kitty didn't know how many hours – passed in the Wilderness, but no sign of night arrived to save her from the sun, which scorched her skin; a biblical punishment for a woman who had very little faith left in her. The silence engulfed her, with not even the cry of a wild animal to break the spell. No birds flew in the sky, no snakes crawled along the ground, and no cactus reared its spikes up to the blistering hot sky. She supposed she would die soon, and she beckoned death to her on that first day. Frank had left her desolate, but not even that compared to the utter desolation around her.

This was it. This was the Wilderness. With growing horror she realised she was the only living thing there.

Anne was finishing up her report on Kitty's exile when one of the warders came bursting into her office.

"There's something wrong with Mags. They're taking her to the facility."

"What's happened?"

"I don't know. She was talking one minute. Loud and vulgar, like she always does. Next minute she's slumped on the floor."

Anne followed the warder to the facility, where Mags lay curled up in a foetal position on one of the gurneys. Her bulky body burst through the safety barriers on either side.

"We'll have to do more tests, but we can't reach her," said the doctor. "She's catatonic."

"Keep me informed. She's due to be going home next week."

Anne wasn't surprised to find she didn't care about Mags. Some of the women moved her with the stories of hardship, but Mags gave off the glow of pure evil.

The rock was the first thing Kitty managed to move. It had irritated her because the more she tried to walk towards it, the further away it seemed, always just out of reach. Why she should need the rock, she didn't know, but she had a feeling about it that she wanted to prove. Like her feeling that the helicopter ride was something she'd dreamed.

She concentrated on bringing the rock to her. To begin with her mind jarred with the strain, leaving her with a stinking headache for the rest of the day. Not that there was anything but day in this place. That was something else that bothered her. She wasn't an expert on the movement of the sun and moon, but she was sure there should be a few hours of night.

THE PAPER GARDEN   SALLY QUILFORD

It took her several days – as she counted them – and lots of headaches before the rock finally edged towards her. The first time it bounced right back, so she tried again, until it came, albeit slowly, leaving a trail in its wake. Finally she could touch it, and assure herself it was real.

Anne Sullivan had barely finished her lunch when she got the call from Rav.

"Something is happening to Kitty," he said. "I hadn't noticed it, because of all the new exiles. We've sent a dozen to the Wilderness since Kitty, and they're all reacting badly. Hiro over at the facility thinks that some might have to be taken out for a while, then returned when we know what the problem is."

"Yes, I've heard. I'll leave that decision to the Board. What about Kitty?"

"She's moved the rock."

"So?" Anne didn't understand.

"Only we can manipulate the things in the Wilderness. That's not all."

"What else?"

"There are some other objects there, that we can't identify. The computer isn't picking them up. That's still not all."

"Dare I ask?"

"She's got company."

She wanted something more interesting to look at than the rock. No real flowers would grow here, so Kitty thought hard. Within five minutes, where her water and bread normally landed, there was a sheet of paper. Not just any sheet of paper. This one – because she wanted the flowers to be large – laid out some three metres square.

Roses, daffodils, and the flowers that had no name but which Kitty had started making as a child, began to decorate the Wilderness.

It was only then that Kitty began to realise the power she held. Mags was just the first. She wondered if she could bring her children, but even if they'd been alive she wouldn't really inflict the Wilderness on them. They'd done nothing wrong, and as much as she needed to see her son and daughter, she didn't think she could bring them back from the dead.

There was one other who deserved to be in the Wilderness with her.

The streets of the Reservation were no place for a woman on her own. They were no place for a man alone. A melting pot of thousands of different races and religions, it had started life as a cosmopolitan city that championed the arts and hosted the commercial centre of the Great Nation. This is what attracted the masses to its golden streets. What it became was a place where no one wanted to live, not even the people who lived there. Nevertheless, Anne returned, to find out about Kitty.

Men and women meandered along the sidewalks, looking for somewhere to score, whilst pasty-faced children played *Gangstas and Dealas.* Just as Anne drove past one group of children, the bad guy – a cop interfering with the important work of the gangstas and dealas – fell to the floor in a hail of bullets. Anne was relieved to see foam missiles bouncing off his tattered t-shirt.

If Anne were more cynical, she might suggest it suited the Great Nation to keep these people here in substandard housing, dependent upon drink and drugs, whilst education was largely ignored in shabby schools that lacked the basic facilities needed to teach a child. After all, drunk, stoned and ignorant people didn't tend to question the decisions made by the government. Here was a different sort of desolation to that found in the Wilderness. A desolation of the mind and the soul. Anne might say that, if she were stupid, but even she knew that whilst the Great Nation insisted on its people having freedom of speech, it was also prone to putting the people who spoke out on lists. Being on a list could have a marked effect on someone's career and lifestyle.

She found Kitty's home deep into the reservation, far from the reasonably respectable homes on the outskirts; built there by the Great Nation to show that there were no slums in the Reservation. That wasn't the impression Anne got from the putrid smelling tenements some sixty blocks in. They huddled together, as if hiding an even dirtier secret behind their crumbling façade.

"Frank?" said the corpulent owner of a corner store. "Haven't seen Frank for weeks. Not since just after his Kitty was taken away." The man spat on the floor, as if Kitty's name had left a vile taste in his mouth. Anne shuddered, knowing that she should feel the same distaste for a woman who killed her children, yet unable to, because living in a place like this could turn anyone into a murderer. "Their apartment is in that building across the way. Fourth floor."

"Yes, I know which apartment it is, thanks."

A few minutes later, Anne was hammering on the door of Frank Turner's apartment. A woman answered, slovenly and heavily pregnant, with greasy blonde hair and filthy fingernails. Kitty, despite her surroundings, had kept herself very clean. The anger Anne suppressed all the way into the slums rose in her chest, threatening to suffocate her.

"Frank ain't well," the woman told Anne.

Anne pushed her way past. It was the only way to behave in this place.

"I told you, he ain't well. He's been asleep for days." Frank sat slumped on the sofa, his head in his knees, having fallen asleep just where he lay.

"Have you called a doctor?"

"I ain't got no money for a doctor. Can't earn any either." The woman pointed to her bump. "Men won't touch me like this."

Anne lifted Frank's head and opened one eye, which stared back at her, rheumy and blank. It was as she suspected. Just like Mags he was in a catatonic state. She made a call on her cell phone, asking for an ambulance.

"I want him taken to the prison," said Anne.

"Hey," said the woman. "He ain't done nothing wrong."

"We need to study him."

"I tell yer, he ain't done nothing wrong. She said he did it, didn't she? That he killed the kids? There's no one can prove it, so you keep away from him. He might have spanked them a little, but he ain't taken no axe to them. I bet she said he made her take the fall, didn't she? She's a liar. Anyways, there's nothing you can do now. She's gone to the Wilderness, ain't she? No one comes back from there, so why upset things by trying to make out she didn't do it?"

The little speech told Anne everything she'd suspected. She only hoped it wasn't too late to bring Kitty back.

"Get out of my way," said Anne, pushing the callous girl aside. She needed to get out of the place. "And don't you try and stop them taking him when they arrive or I'll have you arrested and sent to the Wilderness!" She reached the door and turned back. "You've had a lucky escape. Your baby might have been the next one to be butchered." Wondering if the girl would even notice or care, Anne stormed down the stairs, too angry to wait for the lift.

As she reached the bottom of the stairs, an old woman stumbled through the door, clutching a bottle of booze that smelled more like gasoline. Anne almost knocked her over in her rush to leave the building.

"Annie? My Annie?" said the woman, looking up at Anne with dull eyes. "You've come home?" Thin hands, lined with heavy blue veins and hundreds of liver spots clutched Anne's arm.

"No," said Anne. "You must have me mixed up with someone else. I'm not from around here. I'm not!" With that, she pushed her mother aside before going out into the street and vomiting on the sidewalk.

"Kitty's gone," Hiro told Anne when she arrived at the facility a few hours later. "We've lost her."

"What do you mean, gone?" asked Anne. "I thought we had complete control over her."

"No. Somehow she's escaped the Wilderness."

"Then bring her back. I've got good reason to believe she's innocent."

"We can't, Anne. We've tried. Usually we can bring them back, like when someone is acquitted on a late appeal. Not this time. She's escaped and we can't touch her."

Anne looked down at Kitty's prostrate body, lying on a gurney, hooked up to a life support system, amongst hundreds of other gurneys in the vast facility where hardened criminals were fed the drugs that kept them in the wilderness. Mags had been placed one side of her, with Frank on the other side.

"I'll call the authorities..."

"No," said Anne, holding up her hand to Hiro. "No. They'll want to study her. She wouldn't survive their probing. No one need know about this. Her body is still in our custody, so it doesn't matter where else she might be. If they ask, I'll say I'm studying her, so that we can better understand how someone might escape the Wilderness."

"That's a dangerous game, Anne."

"I'm prepared to play it. Go and see to the others. I want a moment alone with her."

She waited until Hiro was out of earshot and then bent down to whisper in Kitty's ear. "I don't blame you, Kitty. I wish I could escape from the Reservation too, but it still owns me. It will always own me. I hope that wherever you are, you're happy." She kissed Kitty's head, and that was when she felt herself being dragged downwards.

A moment or two later she stood hand in hand with Kitty among giant paper flowers, which had been inelegantly coloured in with what appeared to be crayon. There were roses and daffodils, amongst other flowers so breathtakingly beautiful and unique that they could only have existed in Kitty's imagination. Paper grass grew up from the ground, and far in the distance a paper summerhouse twinkled invitingly in the sunlight. The faint breeze through the garden made Anne think of reading her favourite books, turning the page to hurry on each new adventure, or opening the letter that first told her she'd won a scholarship and could leave the Reservation. All those moments, all those memories were carried in the gentle rustle of the paper.

"I won't keep you here, Miss Sullivan," Kitty said to her. "You don't deserve to be trapped in a place like this. I just wanted you to see."

At the end of the row of flowers stood two statues: Mags and Frank. Kitty had trapped their bodies in plaster, whilst their eyes surveyed yet could not share the wonders that lay before them. Anne turned away, any pity she might have felt dispersed by the memory of their brutal acts against others.

"It's beautiful," said Anne, as she gazed up to the sky. "Beautiful. I wish I could stay." Despite her words, she knew that she wouldn't stay. She wasn't ready to escape yet. Anne took a final languid look at the paper flowers and the paper trees, whilst in the sky above them flew paper birds. Paper animals gambolled among the plants. And running towards Kitty, their arms outstretched, came two paper children.

Copyright © Sally Quilford 2011

INDEFINITY   RICHARD D. FINDLAY

The trees stand tall, terrible omnipotent beings with creaky limbs. Their branches are reaching out accusingly, scraping at my shoulders and legs, as I pound down the track. The sky is bland and overcast, the unfinished water-colour of a student artist. The weather is neither hot nor cold, although sweat seeps through my hair, to trickle over my skin. As I run, my mind inevitably returns to the events that have led me to this point. It seems that all I have ever experienced has conspired to bring me here, where the green of nature infuses everything with layers of myriad shades, and the smell is of freshly dug earth. The track heads off through the trees, forking occasionally. I take the left path every time, curious to find where it leads. I have heard that these paths are called desire lines, and are caused by the constant erosion of human feet on the forest floor; a desire to travel the path of least resistance. I can see her face in the rough bark of the trees, and pick out her silhouette in the bumps and hollows of moss. As I think of her, a discharge of pain and pleasure courses through my body, rushing through my sinews, to make my brain throb.

She had made everyone else fade away with that smile. Her eyes searched mine, and I was drawn to her like lips to chocolate. I remember feeling nervous as I asked her to dance. I had sneakily wiped my sweaty hands on my trousers, in an effort to get rid of my clammy fear. I could feel myself shrivel in the heat of her attention. In contrast, she seemed relaxed and at ease, like some magnificent feline, confident in its territory. Later, she claimed she was as nervous as me. How I laughed when she told me that. I don't think she realised the extent of my hormone fuelled emotions, or the power she had over me that night. I was bewitched.

   She was a graceful mover, but I didn't realise it at the time; I spent that first dance watching my own clumpy feet, and trying my best to ignore the warm-firm feel of her, beneath that slippery silk gown. She told me her name was Lillian, and from that moment, her name became the sound that seemed to encompass all the happiness I felt. In time, we became each other, trading our traits and idiosyncrasies in a game of faith and love. We tried each one on as if they were favourite old shirts, not the habits and pleasures that formed our personalities. We thought that we could make ourselves closer to each other by assimilating ourselves. So in love we became, that she was my universe, and I was hers. We orbited each other, held together by the gravity of our feelings. We lived happily ever onward.

My feet are aching with the metronomic thump. The stab of pain in my shins, that comes with each stride, provides a time frame to measure my thoughts against. The track is unchanging. I have no idea how long I have been running, or how far I have run. I wonder where my watch is. It is one of my most treasured possessions. Engraved on the silver back plate is a message; 'To Victor, with love, Lillian.' I used to take the watch off, just to check the legend was still there, and hadn't somehow worn away. I slog on, hungry and sore. The trees are still towering over me, their crowns framed by the grey beyond. They don't seem quite as menacing now, but I may have just developed a tolerance of them. They seem almost serene at times. I am settled in a steady rhythm, with the sting in my shins and ankles pulsing to my heartbeat. My thoughts are made from the memories she helped me create. I would feel tranquil but for the guilt that bubbles below the surface of me.

The thing I remember most is the expression on her face when she caught me. Her beauty was twisted, misshapen by betrayal, shock, and horror. It was as if my transgression had physically affected her appearance. She had come home from work, feeling unwell. My secretary was on her knees in our living room, her head in my lap.

  I thought she would leave me, but after a while, the screaming and threats died away. I was amazed. It was as if my inability, or unwillingness, to say no, had knocked her vivacity right out of her. Over the weeks and months, her spark gradually fizzled out, as if I had strangled an essential part of her being. As she faded, some part of my unconscious psyche recognised that she was wholly vulnerable, and I began to prey on her insecurities. I used insult and blame, to mould her, to be more receptive to my wants. It was not deliberate, but I somehow slowly, insinuatingly managed to lower her expectations of me and of life. In due course, she eventually distanced herself from her friends and family. I'm not sure if that was my doing, or if she simply stopped caring. Over time, she became totally dependent on me. I'm not proud of what I did, but it's just how it happened. I liked to drink, and maybe that was a contributing factor, but if I'm honest with myself, I became an ugly, nasty soul. Our sex life was pretty much whatever I demanded, and it included ritual humiliation. I also felt it was excusable for me to fuck every tart in a short skirt, within a hundred mile radius, just because I could. In the space of four years, I systematically destroyed her. I should have noticed she was depressed, but she had stopped being *someone* to me. She was a *thing* that existed for my use.

My calves burn with the steady torture. The forest floor is too sharp. I am naked; attempting to merge with the forest. Loping barefoot on pine needles and razor stone. The pain is bright white light. It is all encompassing. My feet and legs are pounded, punished. There is blood on my hands. Where did it come from? Trees are close on either side. I have lost my direction. I keep moving. Where am I going? When did I become so ignorant? Panic froths. Fear percolates. Sweat slicks my skin. My lungs smoulder. Not enough air. Suffocating. Asphyxiating. Too hot. Thoughts are drifting. Her face swims. Hard to focus. Where is Lillian? My eyes are closed. Still I run.

Our last night together, I had been out on the town. I had been a man on a mission, mixing my drinks, and downing them fast. My memories consist of loosely connected scenes in a selection of generic pubs. They are in no particular order, but the order has no relevance anyway. I know I had failed to pull some dizzy blonde, and I was angry she had seen through my patter. I had lurched home with a greasy kebab to keep me company. By this time, we slept in separate rooms. She claimed I was a snorer. She still usually did what I wanted to in bed though; slipping away once I had finished. I staggered up the stairs, and headed straight for her room. I can remember the surprise when she told me no. I can also remember the horrible weeping and sobbing as I held her down and did it anyway. Towards the end she was snarling. Reduced to some weak and helpless animal, hating me. The look of sheer abhorrence that radiated from her actually scared me then, penetrating my drunkenness, and I left her to her tears. My next memory is an odd sensation. I felt pain, but it took several seconds to realise what was happening. I choked and sputtered, but I could get no words out. The fear came as I recognised the knife in my throat. The handle she gripped with white knuckles was familiar. It was a steak knife I had used often. A strange detachment settled over me as she cut through my carotid artery, her hand sawing back and forth as the knife bit deeper still. I saw my own heartbeat reflected in the rhythmic spurt of blood that painted the bedclothes. There was an impression that I was being turned inside out, and I was briefly weightless. I have yet to see heaven or hell.

ZASTI-DORASTI   SUZ WINSPEAR

I still see that place in my dreams, and the terrible look of hatred in those eyes. I can never go back there, of course. I'll never know the truth. After what happened, someone put a high corrugated metal fence all around the garden to stop anyone else getting in, and the whole property disappeared sometime in the late eighties housing boom. There's a complete development of executive houses on the site of what used to be a single old house with a big garden. So it's all lost, the house itself along with any chance of finding an explanation for what happened to Veronica. Or an explanation for the thing that I saw, back in 1976, in the heat of that legendary summer.

Veronica was my cousin. She was three years older than me, but somehow she always seemed much younger. It wasn't her fault. She was an only child, and her parents were elderly. Well, they *seemed* elderly at the time. They were probably only in their fifties when she was a teenager, which is no age at all these days, but it was all very different then. They remembered the War, and the world before the War. Being naturally conservative, naturally insular, that had become their ideal, a heroic innocent unreal England, uncontaminated by American vulgarity or cultural change. They had their standards, and they stuck to them, whether that fitted in with the world outside or not. That made it hard for poor Veronica. They expected her to behave like a child in a 1930s children's book, even when she was in her teens, and got angry if she showed signs of being touched by the modern world. I felt sorry for her. I remember when I was a little girl, going round to her house. Her parents always seemed so strict, she always looked unhappy, and there were so *many* rules! She was never allowed any comics, she never got to watch ITV or eat fish fingers, and the only music I ever heard in that house was light orchestral, or the dreadful 'Sing Something Simple' on a Sunday teatime. The rest of us had pop music! We had comics and loud cartoons! We had fun! So Veronica always seemed to be apart from real life, kept sheltered from the world. Her mother chose her clothes, her shoes and her hairstyle. They were all ugly and marked her out as 'different'. Well, kids these days wouldn't stand for it, would they? But back then . . . Things were different. It wasn't so long ago, but it feels like another world!

Veronica wasn't happy at school. How could she be? The other children teased her and laughed at her, with all the unconscious cruelty of the playground. You could see her yearning to join in with the things that everyone else did, but she always ended up alone. And *that* was when Zasti-Dorasti put in an appearance. She said he first came to her when she was six years old. I don't remember that far back, of course, but from my first memory of her, he was always there. The classic Imaginary Friend. She said that he was a boy, a few years older than she was, with black hair, dressed all in black, and wearing a silver brooch in the shape of a rose. It was a bit of a mystery how a six year old could have thought up so many curious details and such a peculiar name. She talked to him constantly, and insisted that we all say hello to him. She even begged her parents to set a place for him at table, although they never did. She and he played together all the time, and she never seemed to get bored with his company. He was her closest friend. Perhaps her only friend, if truth be told. Yes, I was her cousin, but I was no nicer to her than any of the other kids. All I saw was this odd little girl with over-strict parents and an imaginary friend. Only looking back do I understand what childhood must have been like for her. No wonder she needed Zasti-Dorasti's company so much!

Her parents, of course, hated Zasti-Dorasti.

"There must be something wrong with you!" her mother kept saying, and was always shouting at her, telling her not to be silly, and not to talk to herself because it made people think she was funny in the head. Eventually Veronica stopped acknowledging Zasti-Dorasti in front of them. She didn't mention him, and pretended he wasn't there. But that didn't mean that he'd gone away. She just learned to be discreet about him.

Veronica grew up, and reached that age at which she started to get interested in boys and fashion and pop music. But all these things were strictly forbidden in her parents' house. I remember she kept copies of *Jackie* hidden in her desk at school as though it were some dangerous subversive tract, and I often saw her gazing at pictures of the fashions and the make-up she would never be allowed to wear, and the photos of the pop stars who were creatures of such overwhelming glamour to her, so far from any possible future that she could see for herself.

And so we come to that marvellous hot summer of 1976, the year of the heatwave and the drought. I remember the strange sensation of melting tarmac sticking to the rubber soles of my plimsolls, and seeing the cracked dry yellow ground on the common where there should have been grass. I was 13, a sharp little streetwise kid. I'd already had my first fag round the back of the school. It's nothing much compared to what kids do now, but it was a big rite of passage in those days. Veronica was 16, but in many ways still just a gawky naive child, as alone in the world as ever, all awash with longings and hopelessness.

She came over to my house one Sunday. I can't remember why she was allowed to visit us on her own – her parents considered me a bad influence. There must have been a reason, but as I say, I can't remember it. My mother got us a Chinese takeaway for lunch, which was a real treat for Veronica, as she was never allowed any 'foreign' food at home. Afterwards

ZASTI-DORASTI   SUZ WINSPEAR

when the two of us were sitting under the apple tree in the garden, too hot to move, I asked her if Zasti-Dorasti was still around.

"Oh yes!" said Veronica. "He's always around. He's here now, sitting just over there. He's always with me."

She looked aside and smiled at the empty air, as though at a friendly face.

"Still a little boy, is he? Like he was when you used to talk about him?"

"Of course not! He's grown up! . . . He's beautiful! More beautiful than anyone you've *ever* seen! More beautiful than Freddie Mercury, even! He's got lovely pure white skin, and jet black hair, and his eyes are *so* blue! I've never *seen* eyes as blue as that! And he always dresses in black and wears a silver brooch in the shape of a rose . . . And he's my friend! *My* friend! . . . He talks to me, you know. He tells me the most wonderful things about places he goes to, places that most people don't even know exist. Sometimes he sings to me. His voice is so beautiful! Sometimes I think I'll go mad if I don't hear it all the time . . .And you know what? One day, he's going to come and rescue me. He told me. He said he'll take me away, and I'll never have to come back here. Never! He'll come and get me. Take me away! Then I'll have beautiful clothes, and we'll go to all these wonderful places he's told me about! We'll go there together, and I'll see everything I've ever dreamed of, and I'll look into those blue eyes every day . . . It won't be like this place. It won't be like school. It's going to be *wonderful*!"

She lay back and looked up through the branches of the apple tree at the perfect cloudless sky, and scowled for a moment, as though comparing its colour unfavourably with Zasti-Dorasti's brilliant eyes.

"Let's go somewhere," I said, thinking that all this talk of Zasti-Dorasti was beginning to get a bit weird. I mean, he was beginning to sound like something a bit more than an imaginary friend.

"Go somewhere?" she said, sitting up. "Where?"

"Oh, I don't know . . . just somewhere."

"Alright," she said. "We'll have to ask your mother . . ."

"We don't *have* to," I said. "She doesn't mind me going out."

"What? On your own?"

"Yes. She doesn't mind. She lets me go anywhere."

So we went out the back gate and down the alley to the street. Now I told Veronica we weren't going anywhere in particular, but in fact there *was* somewhere I'd been wanting to go for ages, but just hadn't wanted to go there on my own. A couple of streets from where I lived was this enormous old house, half ruined in a big overgrown garden. There had been a terrible fire there once, or so I'd been told, and after the fire it had simply been abandoned. Nobody knew who owned it. Me and the local kids, we'd been daring one another to go in there all summer, but so far nobody had done it because the house was so scary. The story was going around that the people who died in the fire were still there, haunting the place, and that nobody who went in ever came out. You know the sort of silly rumours that children tell and spread. But Veronica didn't know these stories so I thought I'd be able to get her to come with me . . . It seemed like a good idea at the time.

We got to the brick wall that surrounded the house, and to the wood that boarded up the gateway. It was rotting, parts had fallen down, and there were a couple of places where you could squeeze through quite easily. Veronica didn't want to go in. She said we'd be trespassing and it wasn't right of us. That was how she'd been brought up. But I shoved her through anyway, even though she was bigger than me and her clothes got caught a couple of times, and we were there in the tangled wilderness of the garden before she could kick up too much of a fuss.

She liked the garden. *That* surprised me. I found it a bit creepy. All the bushes had gone wild; there was a bamboo forest to get lost in, a ruined greenhouse full of broken clay pots, and a tumbledown old summerhouse with hundreds of spiders crawling in dirty webs inside its wooden roof. But Veronica just ran about the garden laughing, and insisted on exploring all the darkest and creepiest places. She wanted to see everything! Maybe she felt free in there. Nobody could see her, apart from me. Nobody could tell her off. There weren't any rules in the wilderness, were there? No-one to tell her what to do.

Then we came to the house. Even in the heat, it felt oddly chilly there. I could see that the glassless window frames were all scorched and turned to charcoal, and there was just a heap of burnt stuff where the front door used to be.

"Let's go in!" I whispered to Veronica.

"Oh yes!" she said. "*Let's!*"

I'd never known her to be so enthusiastic about anything before! Veronica, who was afraid to walk through the school playground for fear of teasing, who was intimidated by her strict parents and by everyone else she knew, wasn't scared in the least! Suddenly I was glad I'd chosen her to come with me. Cause I couldn't show myself to be scared in front of her, could I? So I had to look tough even if I felt like running away.

We went into the hallway. The fire had evidently been at its worst here; there was nothing but scorched brick walls, with no plaster left. No ceiling either. We could look straight up through the blackened roof-beams directly at the sky. The tiles had gone a long time ago, and the contrast of the beams in dark silhouette against the brilliant blue sky was astonishing.

We went further inside, tiptoeing over the blackened debris on the floor, which smeared our shoes with ash. And we found a part of the house that wasn't quite so badly damaged. In some sheltered places, long strips of charred wallpaper remained clinging to the walls, and there were a few things among the wreckage, pieces of wooden furniture turned to charcoal, a china cup, a metal lamp-standard, that were still quite recognisable.

Now at this point I started to feel a little bit weird. Things that were recognisable – they started to seem a bit too close to the people who had owned them. I could imagine these rooms with all their furniture in them, and all the ordinary little things that people keep around themselves, and I could imagine the room burning, everything being destroyed. Even now, when our feet stirred the ash, there was a faint scent of burning. That image of destruction frightened me. Maybe people had died in this room, by the charred table, or sitting among the frame and springs which were all that was left of an armchair. There was a thing of burnt wood and twisted metal that I realised must have been an old-fashioned gramophone. Someone had listened to music on that once. Maybe they had worn beautiful dresses and danced and fallen in love in this room.

"I want to go back now," I said. My fake courage had finally failed me.

"No!" said Veronica. "Not yet! This is *fun*!"

She spoke like someone who'd never had fun before, experiencing it for the very first time. Like the first time getting drunk.

And then something caught her eye. She gave a little gasp, then reached down into the rubbish on the floor and picked it up.

"Look!" she shrieked. "*Look!*"

"What is it?" I said.

"This brooch. It's Zasti-Dorasti's brooch!"

She held it out for me to see, and I took it from her. It was, as she had said, a silver brooch in the shape of a rose. Only it wasn't the bright sparkling piece of jewellery that I'd always imagined. It had been through the fire, and it was tarnished and crushed. A leaf had broken off, and the pin at the back had twisted so that it barely did up properly.

"Yeah, right," I said. "It's just an old brooch!"

"No, this is it! *This* is exactly what it looks like!"

"What, like that? All broken?"

"Yes. Just like this."

And then Veronica snatched back the brooch, turned around and began to run further into the house. I called to her to come back, but either she ignored me or she couldn't hear. I raced after her, though by that stage I really didn't want to see any more of that house. But I didn't want to be left on my own there either. She ran into a big room, just as burnt and wrecked as all the others, and I was a few steps behind her.

Maybe this had been a ballroom once, I thought. It had a series of French windows, empty now of glass, all down one side. It must have been facing west, as the afternoon sunlight shone right in through every window, casting harsh shadows of the empty window frames over the rubble-strewn floor. Veronica stood there among the fallen wreckage of a chandelier that was strewn across the floor, the broken crystals catching the sunlight with random sparkles and flashes of colour, and she began to speak out loud.

"I'm so glad! I knew you'd come! I *knew*! I *always* knew! At last! . . . We'll never come back, will we? We'll see such wonderful things!"

She reached out as though holding the hand of someone. Someone invisible. Her face was glowing with sheer joy. I had never seen anybody look so happy! Not before then, not since then. She was quite simply overwhelmed with happiness.

"Veronica! Stop it!" I shouted, suddenly afraid of what was happening. "You're being all weird!"

I picked up a lump of wood from the charred parquet of the floor and threw it at the place where the invisible person seemed to be. It hit the ground with a clunk, and sent up a small cloud of dust and ash. As the sunlight poured through the empty windows, it caught this dust and made every mote glint black and gold amidst the gleams of the smashed crystals. And in the dust and that strange glitter, I could see a shape, a human shape that could never have been seen in normal light, not entirely part of the physical world, not a thing of flesh and blood. It was a graceful young man dressed entirely in black, a crushed silver brooch in the shape of a rose shining dully on his lapel. He turned and looked at me. This was no fairytale prince. This was something that had never been human. What I saw was a porcelain-white face of uncanny androgynous beauty, with eyes just as blue as the sky outside. They seemed to shine with an eerie light of their own. He looked at me, and his expression wasn't friendly. Maybe it was because I'd thrown the wood at him. But I don't think it was. I think he knew just how many times I had teased Veronica, and how often I had laughed at her behind her back. He knew what a false friend I had been to her. And the look he gave me was one of pure malice . . .

I ran. My instinctive sense of self-preservation took over. I left Veronica in her happiness, I left Zasti-Dorasti, or whatever that thing was, and I ran away, tripping on the filthy rubble underfoot, desperate to get out of that house.

I ran straight home, back to the ordinary world where things like that don't happen. My mother was beginning to wonder where I'd got to. When she saw me, on my own, with my feet, legs and clothes all black with charcoal smears, she suddenly got worried. She asked me what had happened.

I lied. Or rather, I told *bits* of the truth. Now that the fear had worn off a little, now that I was safe in the real world, I had started to think about what to tell people, and I knew what people would believe. And what they wouldn't believe. I didn't want my friends to think I'd gone a bit weird. I didn't want them to tease me.

I said I'd suggested to Veronica we go for a walk. But then I said that *she* had made me go into the burnt house. That she forced me. And that I had run away because I didn't want to go in any further.

My mother and a couple of neighbours went to search for Veronica. They didn't find her, so they called the police. They found her shoes, but that was all. They didn't find her clothes, or anything else of her. She simply disappeared that afternoon. There was no sign of her. No sign whatsoever. Her parents came over and shouted at me a lot, but I couldn't tell them anything. I certainly wasn't going to tell them what I'd seen. They wouldn't have believed me anyway, and they were so angry that I was afraid to tell them the truth. What would they have said if I'd told them that Zasti-Dorasti was real? After that, they had a big row with my parents, and they never spoke to my mother again, so I didn't hear anything else. What I do know is that Veronica never came back. I think Zasti-Dorasti took her away just as she told me he would. Whether she's now dressed in beautiful clothes, seeing wonderful places, well I'll never know, will I? But I am certain that Zasti-Dorasti is still out there somewhere. And from that malicious look in his terrifying eyes, I know that whatever sort of being he really is, Zasti-Dorasti hates me.